"Protection is my job, and I know I blew it before, but I'm not going to make that mistake again."

Her lashes fluttered against her smooth cheeks. "I wasn't in any danger when you left me to do another tour."

"You were in danger of erecting your hard shell again. I'd broken through. I'd made you feel safe and loved, and then I snatched all that away." He skimmed the pad of his thumb along her jaw. "And I never even said I was sorry."

"You did what you had to do." She shrugged, and he put his hands on her raised shoulders.

"Don't. Don't pretend it didn't hurt. Don't pretend I didn't betray your trust, your...love."

Her chest rose and fell as she twisted her fingers in her lap. "Liam, I..."

He held his breath, waiting for the words he'd needed to hear from her two years ago.

Instead an explosion rocked the car and lit up the night sky.

NAVY SEAL SPY

CAROL ERICSON

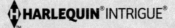
HARLEQUIN® INTRIGUE®

For LRF, my future Navy SEAL

ISBN-13: 978-0-373-69862-2

Navy SEAL Spy

Copyright © 2015 by Carol Ericson

Printed in U.S.A.

www.Harlequin.com

Carol Ericson lives with her husband and two sons in Southern California, home of state-of-the-art cosmetic surgery, wild freeway chases and a million amazing stories. These stories, along with hordes of virile men and feisty women, clamor for release from Carol's head. It makes for some interesting headaches until she sets them free to fulfill their destinies and her readers' fantasies. To learn more about Carol, please visit her website, carolericson.com, "Where romance flirts with danger."

Books by Carol Ericson

Harlequin Intrigue

Brothers in Arms: Retribution

Under Fire
The Pregnancy Plot
Navy SEAL Spy

Brody Law

The Bridge
The District
The Wharf
The Hill

Brothers in Arms: Fully Engaged

Run, Hide
Conceal, Protect
Trap, Secure
Catch, Release

Guardians of Coral Cove

Obsession
Eyewitness
Intuition
Deception

Harlequin Intrigue Noir

Toxic

Visit the Author Profile page at Harlequin.com for more titles.

CAST OF CHARACTERS

Liam McCabe—A covert ops agent and former navy SEAL who runs into his ex-fiancée while working undercover and must choose between protecting her and accepting the help only she can give.

Katie O'Keefe—A computer hacker who has her own reasons for working undercover gets more than she bargains for when she discovers her ex-fiancé is employed by the same agency. Can she ignore the man who broke her heart, or will she wind up getting them both killed?

Sebastian Cole—A former Tempest agent who commits suicide, prompting his closest friend to find answers.

Garrett Patterson—His death confirms Katie's suspicions about her employer...and puts her own life in danger.

Ginger Spann—This tightly wound executive has special plans for Katie that may facilitate her access to Tempest's secrets, but will also place her firmly in the eye of the storm.

Mr. Romo—The man in charge of the Tempest training facility has a weakness for strong women, which just might lead to his demise.

Samantha Van Alstyn—Katie's coworker pays the price for a case of mistaken identity.

Dustin Gantt—This recruit's suspicious behavior has Liam wondering if he's friend or foe.

Caliban—The mysterious leader of Tempest, the black ops organization that's trying to throw world affairs into chaos, wants to rule the world and satisfy his vendetta against Jack Coburn and Prospero in the process.

Chapter One

A soft footfall outside the door raised the hair on the back of Katie's neck. With her gaze riveted to the dull silver handle of the door, she watched it go down slowly and then click against the lock.

She spun around on the toes of her low-heeled shoes and launched toward the closet. Good thing she'd mapped out an escape route days ago after studying the layout of the offices. Of course, the closet would be more like a trap than an escape if someone decided to investigate.

Holding her breath, she slipped into the claustrophobic space and crouched behind some boxes. She had a sliced-up view of the office through the slats on the closet door.

The door to the office swung open, and the figure of a man filled the frame. "I didn't expect to see you here this late."

Her heart slammed against her chest, and she rocked back on her heels with her rehearsed excuse running through her head.

A woman answered from the hallway. "I forgot some papers in my office and wanted to do some work at home. What's your excuse?"

The blood rushed to Katie's head, and she planted her hand against a box to steady herself. She pressed her other hand against her mouth to stifle her panting breath. Of course, nobody could see her through the slats and behind the boxes—yet.

The man, Garrett Patterson, responded. "I thought I'd left my office door unlocked and came back to check it out. I had no intention of doing any more work, unlike some people. You work too hard, Ginger. Do you ever turn off that brain of yours?"

Ginger Spann's tinkling laugh sounded close. She must've entered the room behind Garrett.

"Just like a man to think a woman has to turn off her brain to relax or…enjoy herself."

The door to the office clicked shut, and the soft sounds of rustling material floated across the room.

Katie swallowed, poked her head out from behind a box and squinted through the slats on the closet door. She couldn't see heads, only bodies, and those bodies were doing some naughty things to each other.

If she wasn't in hiding, she could record this encounter and turn it over to Human Resources—if they had an HR department and if she was a snitch. Neither was the case.

As Garrett pushed Ginger against the desk, she groaned, and Katie almost groaned along with her. How long would she be trapped here while these two went at it?

Garrett murmured. "I never thought you were interested before, even though I tried my damnedest to entice you. I've been waiting a long time for this, Ginger."

"Mmm, so have I, Garrett. So have I."

Someone gasped. Garrett? Who knew cold, uptight Ginger Spann had the moves to bring a man like Garrett to his knees?

Garrett slumped across the desk, and Katie drew back from her peephole as his face appeared in her line of sight. His mouth gaped open, and his eyes bugged out of their sockets.

What was Ginger doing to him, and could she give lessons?

Then Ginger shifted from beneath Garrett's body and pushed him to the floor, where he fell in a heap, his pale face still turned in Katie's direction.

Katie drove her fist against her mouth. Garrett looked... dead.

Ginger straightened her pencil skirt and smoothed her hands over the fabric. She crouched next to Garrett's body, but Katie couldn't see her face.

Ginger must be in shock. Her movements, slow and deliberate, didn't look like those of someone who'd just had a guy drop dead on top of her.

Katie watched, her mouth dry, as Ginger felt for his pulse. Then Ginger's hand plunged into his pocket.

Katie froze, afraid to move one muscle, as Ginger searched Garrett's body. What the hell was she doing? Why wasn't she calling 911?

When Ginger rose to her feet, Katie gave a silent sigh of relief. Maybe Ginger was just trying to cover her backside—literally. As far as Katie knew, Garrett was a married man. She knew nothing about Ginger's marital status, although rumors had been circulating about her and the big boss. The woman was as cold as an icicle.

Katie heard the tones of cell phone buttons, and her stomach dropped. Once the EMTs swarmed this place, what chance would she have of escaping? It could be hours. She could be discovered.

"We've got a problem." Ginger's sharp tone was a one-eighty from her breathy pillow talk with Garrett. "I got here all right, but Garrett Patterson was here before me."

Ginger paused and then lashed back. "How the hell am I supposed to know? I couldn't risk it. He's dead."

Katie swallowed.

"This is your problem. You're the one who lost your

badge in his office. Send one of your minions over here to help me out. Now."

She must've ended the call because she'd stopped talking. Ginger moved toward the door and out of Katie's sight, but Garrett's dead eyes still stared at her in her hiding place.

Both she and Garrett had stumbled on more than they'd bargained for. Garrett had forgotten to lock his office door when he'd left for the day, and Katie had been careening down the hallway looking for an unlocked door.

Garrett's action had gotten him killed, and hers had gotten her trapped—but had also confirmed her suspicions about her place of work. Now, if she could only get out of this situation alive.

A soft tap on the door had Katie's heart hammering again.

The door opened and Ginger whispered. "Did anyone see you?"

"No. Besides, I have an excuse for wandering the halls at this hour."

"You're an idiot. How did you manage to lose your badge?"

A pair of legs encased in gray pants with a black stripe up the side came into Katie's line of vision. Security.

"My plastic badge holder cracked on one side. It must've fallen out, but at least I figured out where."

"Yeah, you're a real genius. Get a new badge holder. Patterson was already suspicious. Finding your badge in his office would've amped up his suspicions even more."

The security guy whistled and crouched beside Garrett's lifeless body. A hand with a bird tattooed on the back reached for Garrett's throat. "How'd you do him?"

"As far as you're concerned, he had a heart attack."

"With his fly down?" The security guard chuckled.

"That's why you're here. Set it up."

"Fingerprints?"

"Don't worry about fingerprints. I have every right to be in Garrett's office, and nobody's going to be doing a criminal investigation here if you stage it correctly."

The guard hoisted Garrett's body up and dragged him out of Katie's view. Unfortunately, the two conspirators exchanged very few words as they positioned Garrett at his desk and straightened up the office.

Katie hadn't noticed a security guard's badge when she'd first entered Garrett's office, which seemed like hours ago now, but she hadn't known what to look for. It was the first time in two weeks of searching that she'd discovered an unlocked office, and she'd meant to take advantage of it.

If she'd found that badge first, there's no telling what she could've discovered about her employer, Tempest… and Sebastian's suicide.

"That should do it." The security guard cleared his throat. "Should I close his eyes?"

"Why? People die with their eyes open all the time."

"I don't know. He looks kinda…surprised."

"He was."

Katie shivered. Why kill Garrett unless she suspected him of returning to his office to get the security guard's badge? Why would he do that? Was it because he had his own doubts about Tempest?

The security guy's shoes squeaked as he crossed the floor. "Should I discover him tonight?"

"Let someone else discover him tomorrow morning. Keep a low profile."

"He's a married guy. His wife might come looking for him or start calling around."

"Garrett's wife is out of town." Ginger made a clicking noise. "He must've told me that ten times this week."

"Then he's someone else's problem."

Ginger brushed past the closet door, and Katie's heart stuttered as she caught a whiff of Ginger's light, citrus perfume.

"I'm leaving first. Wait at least a minute and then get lost."

"Should I leave the door locked or unlocked?"

"Leave it unlocked—the easier for someone to find him tomorrow morning."

"I hope this works."

"Of course it'll work. I didn't slit his throat. The drug I gave him mimics a heart attack, and that's all you need to know."

The door clicked open and shut, and Katie eased out a short breath. Ginger terrified her—even more now.

The security guard hummed a tuneless song as Katie closed her eyes and counted the seconds until his departure. Her muscles ached with tension.

Just when she thought she'd be holed up in the closet all night, she heard the door open and close and blessed silence descended on the office. Leaning her forehead against the nearest box, she released a noisy sigh.

She shifted her stiff body and pressed her eye against the slat in the door. As far as she could see, the room looked empty, not that she expected Ginger or the security guard to pop out from behind the desk—but she wouldn't put it past them.

Unlike Ginger, she had no reason to be in Garrett Patterson's office, so she shrugged out of her sweater and wiped down the boxes and the inside of the closet door. Still using the sweater, she pushed against the door to open it and crawled out.

She straightened up and then immediately swayed to the side when she caught sight of Garrett slumped in his chair, his eyes still open. She crept toward the desk and reached across the body to shuffle through the contents on top of his blotter. The security guard must've found his badge.

Like most employees at Tempest, Garrett worked on a laptop that he must've already taken home for the evening.

Her fingers tripped across the edge of a notebook shoved beneath the blotter. She pulled it free and thumbed through the pages of what looked like an appointment book.

As she wiped the desk clean with the sweater, it caught on the arm of Garrett's chair and she yanked it free. She didn't want to get any closer to him than she had to.

She shoved her arms into the sleeves and tucked Garrett's spiral notebook into the pocket. Grasping the door handle with the sleeve of the sweater pulled over her hand, she took one last glance at the room. If she'd had her cell phone with her, she could've caught the whole scene on video. Of course, if she'd had her phone with her and it'd buzzed, she could be dead right now.

She pushed down on the handle and inched open the door. The hallway stretched to her right toward the stairwell, and she slipped from the office and tiptoed down the hallway. She'd already checked these other doors earlier—all locked.

When she reached the metal door to the stairwell, she pulled the sleeve of the sweater over her hand again. She didn't think the authorities would be checking for fingerprints out here, but she didn't want to be connected to this floor in any way. She'd already tampered with the security camera, and she'd fix its footage later.

Anxious to put as much distance between herself and Garrett Patterson, she charged through the door. She took the stairs two at a time on her way down and then stumbled to a screeching halt as a man materialized in front of her.

A scream roared from her lungs and then ended in a squeak on her lips as she looked up into the bluest eyes she'd ever seen—or at least the bluest eyes she'd ever seen since the last time she'd locked lips with the man who broke her heart.

Chapter Two

Adrenaline pumped through Liam's body as he reached out to grab the woman barreling into him. She tipped back her head, her perfect lips forming a perfect O, and his adrenaline kicked up another notch.

He whispered the name of the woman who'd been haunting his dreams for two years. "Katie-O."

"You!" Her dark eyebrows collided over her nose. "What the hell are you doing here?"

"Me?" He didn't know whether to give her a shake or a kiss, so he settled for smoothing the pads of his thumbs along her collarbone as he still held her by the shoulders. "What are *you* doing here?"

"Always answering a question with a question." She shrugged him off. "I work here."

His eyes narrowed, and his senses kicked into high alert. "You work for Tempest?"

"Shh. Don't tell anyone. It's top secret." She held her finger to her lips, and her eyes sparkled in the dimness of the stairwell.

He'd never known when to take Katie seriously—that had been one of their many problems during their brief acquaintance. Her dramatic words and gestures were over the top, but they held an ultimate truth. If she did, indeed, work for Tempest, then her work was top secret.

"In what capacity, the recreation adviser?" Last he'd heard, Katie was designing video games.

She removed her finger from her lips and shook it under his nose. "Not so fast. I asked you what you were doing here first."

He studied her face in the low light. She was angry with him about the way they'd ended things. He couldn't trust her. Hell, he couldn't trust anyone.

He lowered his voice and put his lips close to her ear. "What do you think I'm doing here?"

She twitched back from him. "The last time I saw you in San Diego, you had one more tour of duty as a navy SEAL. So, you're either here as a consultant or you're training to be an…agent."

"Brilliant deduction."

"Which is it?" She wedged her hands on her hips, as feisty as ever.

"It's top secret." He winked at her.

The door above them scraped open, and Liam pulled Katie into his arms, lunging for the recessed area between the two sets of stairs. A shaft of light from the hallway crept across the landing above them as the door widened.

A footstep landed on the cement floor, and heavy breathing echoed through the stairwell.

Liam held Katie tighter.

The silky strands of her black hair got caught on the scruff of his beard as he held her head against his chest with one hand. If she wondered why someone's presence in the stairwell had sent him scrambling for cover, her curiosity didn't lead her to break away from him or call out to the stranger.

The intruder shuffled onto the landing as if he was peering down the stairs. Then he backtracked and let the fire door slam shut.

Liam remained still for several more seconds, holding Katie, inhaling the sweet fragrance emanating from her skin.

Still in his arms, she tilted her head back, and he could see the pulse in her throat beating wildly. Had his actions frightened her? Aroused her?

Her voice was a low whisper. "Wh-why did you do that?"

"I'm not sure I'm allowed in this building, and I'm bucking for a perfect training score."

"If you're not supposed to be here, what are you doing in this stairwell?"

"Are you allowed in this building?"

"I work on the first floor."

"What are you doing on the fourth floor?"

She pushed away from him and crossed her arms. "Uh, ladies' room—they're on the even-numbered floors only, and the one on the second floor is out of order."

His gaze dropped to her arms crossed over her chest, her fingers biting into her upper arms. She was lying.

"Then maybe we didn't have to hide. I could've said I was visiting you."

"No!"

The word was out of her mouth before he finished his sentence.

He could almost feel the waves of heat coming from her cheeks as she twirled a lock of hair around her finger. "I—I just think it's better if Tempest doesn't know that we were…acquaintances. Don't you?"

The minute Katie-O had plowed into him, he'd had no intention of revealing his relationship with her to Tempest, and he never would've allowed her to do it, either. The fact that she'd come up with the deception first made his life a lot easier…and made him a lot more suspicious.

He raised his eyes to the ceiling and tapped his chin. "I suppose that's probably for the best. Tempest is a covert agency that forbids you to tell anyone where you work. Is it that way for you, too?"

"Absolutely." She puffed out a breath. "I had to sign all sorts of forms and agreements to keep my employment here under wraps—even from my closest family members."

"Even from Sebastian? He's like a brother to you. I can't imagine you'd keep anything from him."

Her pale skin blanched even more and her huge, dark eyes sparkled with tears. "Sebastian's dead."

Without thinking of anything but taking her hurt away, he gathered her in his arms again. "I'm so sorry, Katie. I hadn't heard."

He hadn't heard much of anything in the past two years since he'd seen her. He'd been deployed for another year in Afghanistan and then immediately plucked from the navy for…another assignment.

She sniffled against his chest but didn't offer up any details. If she didn't want to talk about Sebastian, he didn't want to ask her to elaborate on the death of the man who'd been the only person she'd called family.

"Is that why you took a job with Tempest in the middle of Idaho, to get away from everything?"

Stepping back, she grabbed both of his hands, her nails digging into his flesh. "Don't tell anyone here that you know me."

He'd be more than happy to keep her secret, since that meant she'd be keeping his. "You have my word, Katie."

"And don't—" she flung his hands away from her "—call me Katie."

He opened his mouth to find out what she wanted him to call her, but she spun around and disappeared down the stairwell.

KATIE RAN HER tongue along the inside of her dry mouth as the announcement from the Giant Voice system blared from the speaker in the corner of the office where she shared cubicle space with other employees from various departments.

"All-hands meeting in the building S cafeteria. Report immediately to the building S cafeteria."

Katie removed her access card from her computer and grabbed her purse from the desk drawer. Hooking it over her shoulder, she joined her coworker Samantha in the line of people heading for the office door.

Samantha cupped her hand over her mouth and dipped her head toward Katie. "What do you think this is all about?"

"I have no idea." Katie's gaze ping-ponged among the faces of her other coworkers filing out of the office into the hallway. Their expressions registered everything from boredom to curiosity to fear. The fearful ones, she'd come to realize, were either total newbies like her or long-termers, but she hadn't yet figured out what they had to fear.

"Hey." Samantha tugged on Katie's purse strap. "Do you think all hands include all the hot guys who are over at the gym training every day?"

"I thought we weren't allowed over at the gym."

"Don't be such a Goody Two-shoes, KC. I told you I'd heard there was hot man meat over there, and I was going to check it out." Samantha smacked her lips. "And I'm here to tell you the reports didn't lie."

"You're going to get yourself fired, Samantha." If spying on the agents got Samantha fired, then she couldn't even imagine her punishment for spying on a murder.

Samantha shrugged. "Whatever. This job sucks, anyway. Too many rules, regulations and restrictions, and not a damned thing to do out here in the middle of nowhere."

"The pay's good."

"That's about the only perk." She dropped her voice and moved close to Katie again. "And you can't tell me you think Mr. Romo is anyone who remotely resembles a normal boss."

"Quiet." Katie glanced around at the other Tempest employees streaming into the cafeteria. Maybe Samantha didn't want to keep this job, but Katie had to keep it—even now that Liam had turned up. Maybe even more so.

How had Liam gotten involved with Tempest? She bit her lip and blinked the tears from her eyes. Probably the same way Sebastian had gotten involved, but she hadn't come here to save Liam McCabe.

She came to get justice for Sebastian, and she wouldn't allow anyone to stand in her way—not even Liam.

As she shuffled into the cafeteria, Katie noticed the security guards at each door. She studied their faces, impassive beneath their caps, and wondered which one had helped Ginger last night. If she could get a look at the backs of their hands, she'd know for sure.

"I feel like I should be mooing." Samantha tossed her hair back and then nudged Katie's shoulder. "The man parade is here. This must be important."

Katie jerked her head to the left and watched a line of impressive men, with one woman in their midst, snake through the side door and line up against the wall. Facially, they weren't all handsome, at least not like Liam, who possessed the classic good looks of a California surfer, but all of them had incredible builds with muscles that went on forever and an air of quiet competence. And these were just the new recruits.

Man meat, indeed.

Had Liam picked her out of the crowd as easily as she had him? As she studied his face across the room, he looked up and met her eyes as if he knew exactly where she'd been standing all along.

Closing her eyes, she allowed herself one delicious shiver as she relived their meeting in the stairwell last night and once again felt Liam's arms around her. He'd smelled precisely as she remembered—fresh like an ocean breeze, manly and strong.

Her eyelids flew open. And now he was part of Tempest— the enemy.

Pradeep Singh tapped the microphone at the front of the room, and the other managers lined up behind him. Their boss, Mr. Romo, was absent as usual. Ginger took a position to Pradeep's right, folding her hands loosely in front of her, the business suit, glasses and chignon sending a demure, professional vibe.

But Katie knew better.

"Hello, everyone." Pradeep waved his hands. "There are some seats up front, but we won't keep you too long."

Not many in the crowd took him up on his offer, so he continued.

"I know some of you have been hearing rumors this morning, and some of you early risers heard sirens and may have even seen the ambulance."

Katie swallowed and hung on to her purse strap. *Here it comes.*

Pradeep cleared his throat. "I'm sorry to report that one of our own, Garrett Patterson, died at the compound last night."

A few gasps and oohs and aahs rippled through the room, and Ginger leaned toward Pradeep, covering the mic with her hand as she whispered something in his ear.

Pradeep nodded once. "Garrett had a heart attack in his office last night—in this very building on the fourth floor."

A wave of sympathetic murmurs swirled through the cafeteria, but Katie felt the air brimming with tension. Was it just the fact that a coworker had died in the building, or did the Tempest employees sense something more? She glanced around the room at the concerned and sad faces— emotions totally in keeping with the announcement.

She continued to scan the crowd and like a magnet, her eyes locked on to Liam's. Even from this distance she could feel the intensity of his gaze. He'd probably taken note that Garrett had keeled over on the fourth floor—the floor she'd been exiting when she bumped into him on the stairwell. Liam didn't miss much—except when it came to emotion.

Ginger stepped up to the mic next. "We'll be taking up a collection for flowers for Garrett's wife. The memorial service will be back East, so please pay your respects with a little donation."

Katie clenched her jaw at Ginger's phony, saccharine tone. Pradeep droned on for a bit more, but she'd tuned out. They'd put the heart attack story out there, and apparently had no trouble selling it to the EMTs who'd responded this morning.

Would that be the end of it? Could she phone in an anonymous tip to the police to check for some sort of heart attack-inducing drug?

"Earth to KC." Samantha snapped her fingers in front of Katie's face.

Pradeep had stopped speaking, and the crowd had begun shuffling back to their work areas, talking in low voices.

"Psst." Samantha pinched her arm. "Let's exit the same way the agents are exiting."

"A coworker just died and that's all you can think about?"

"Between you and me—" Samantha looked both ways "—Garrett had a roving eye. The few times I talked to him, he couldn't seem to keep his gaze at eye level, if you know what I mean."

"So he deserves to drop dead at his desk for being a perv?"

"Was he at his desk?" Samantha cocked her head. "I didn't hear them say where he was."

Katie shrugged. "Pradeep said he was found in his office, so I just assumed he was at his desk."

Samantha herded her across the room to the farthest exit door where Liam and the other agents were headed. Would Liam think she was trying to get close to him?

She and Samantha jostled for position, and someone bumped her purse from behind. Gripping the strap, she glanced over her shoulder.

"Sorry." Liam dropped his eyes to her purse and then stared straight ahead as if she was just another Tempest office worker—not someone who'd shared his bed for eight delicious months two years ago.

As the workers fanned out into the hallway, Samantha poked her in the back. "You see? It worked. One of them actually said something to you."

"Yeah, he said sorry for bumping into my purse after you pushed me in front of him."

"Well, that's a start."

"Start of some trouble. We're not supposed to be fraternizing with those guys." Katie flashed her badge at the reader by the office door, and the red light turned to green.

"I'd like to fraternize one or two of them." Samantha winked and then ducked into her cubicle.

Katie dropped into her chair and hunched forward to open her bottom desk drawer to put her purse away. As she wedged it into the drawer, she noticed the corner of a white card sticking out of the side pocket.

Pinching it between two fingers, she pulled it free. The words jumped out at her.

Behind the bleachers at noon.

She recognized the writing as Liam's, and her heart skipped a beat. Should she risk it? She might be able to wheedle some information out of him. She had special ways of handling Liam McCabe—or at least she used to.

She had to find out what he knew. The notebook she'd

snatched from Patterson's office last night had been a bust—just a bunch of abbreviations, a series of numbers and meeting notes.

The rest of the morning crawled by. Samantha popped in to let her know she had to bail on lunch for a meeting with her boss in accounting, which saved Katie from bailing herself.

When the clock on her computer read ten minutes to twelve, Katie grabbed her purse and ducked into the lunchroom to get her sandwich from the fridge. She'd better have some cover for being out at the track on her lunch hour.

Glancing at the gray skies, she turned up the collar of her jacket and crossed the quad. If it started raining, she'd have to abandon the meeting with Liam, and he'd have to reschedule it—or not. What did he want with her, anyway?

She slipped behind the building on the north side of the quad, put her head down and marched toward the gym that had a track behind it. Tempest had taken over an old high school for its compound and had remodeled most of the buildings on campus, even adding dorm-type living quarters for the recruits, but the track and the indoor pool had been maintained.

Employees were allowed to use the gym, but only before and after regular work hours. Tempest wanted to keep the agent recruits and the rest of the employees apart, unless the job directly involved the agents—hers didn't, not yet, anyway.

A few people were jogging around the track, and she realized one of them was Liam. She settled on the second to last row of the bleachers and pulled out her lunch and a book. Ignoring the runners, she ate her sandwich with her book propped open on her knees.

Liam broke away from the track and started jogging up and down the bleachers. On one of his trips down, his pace slowed as he passed her. He panted. "Underneath the bleachers."

She wadded up her brown paper bag and stepped down from the second row. She wandered to the trash can at the back of the bleachers, tossed away her trash and then ducked beneath the bleachers, stepping over the bars criss-crossing the open space. She could still hear Liam's feet as they rang against the metal steps above her.

Less than five minutes later, Liam joined her beneath the bleachers, steam rising from his flesh, damp with sweat. His musky scent pulsed off him in waves, drawing her in, making him seem closer than he was.

His blond hair, away from the sun and surf, had darkened to a burnt gold, but his blue eyes still sparkled like the ocean on a clear day. She curled her hands into fists to squelch the urge to run her fingers through his hair.

"What do you want?" Angry with herself for responding to him in the old familiar ways, her tone came out as harsh as the raw, cold day.

"That guy, Patterson, died in his office on the fourth floor."

She brushed a speck of dirt from the sleeve of her jacket. "Yeah, I know. I was at the same meeting as you."

"You—" he leveled a finger at her "—were on the fourth floor of building S last night, flying down the staircase like you'd seen a ghost."

"Well, I didn't see Garrett Patterson, if that's what you're implying, and if I had, I would've reported his... death instead of chatting about old times with you in the stairwell." She widened her stance and dug her heels into the rubber track beneath her feet.

"Old times? I don't remember any walk down memory lane. You were too busy telling me to keep my mouth shut about knowing you...KC Locke."

"Have you been checking me out?"

His eyes flickered. "If we're going to pull off this pretense, I figured it was best if I knew what you were calling yourself."

"KC Locke." She stuck out her hand. "Nice to meet you."

He took her hand and circled the inside of her wrist with his thumb. "KC, Kathryn Claire Locke—that's the name you used when you were in the foster care system. How does Tempest not know that you started calling yourself Katie and changed your last name to your mother's maiden name, O'Keefe, when you left the system?"

"Shh. I have friends in low places."

"Yeah, more like you used your mad skills with a computer." He tightened his grip on her wrist. "Are you going to tell me what you're doing here under an assumed name?"

She leaned in close just to catch another whiff of him. "I'm going to tell you that Garrett Patterson had a heart attack, and I wasn't there when it happened."

Dropping her hand, he lifted one shoulder. "Don't play with fire, Katie."

"You should've warned me about that two years ago in San Diego." She hunched into her jacket and stepped out from beneath the bleachers.

With her hands stuffed in her pockets and her head down to ward off the chilly wind, she strode toward the track to cross it. Would he come after her? He couldn't. They couldn't be seen together out in the open.

She wandered across the track, sniffing back the tingles in her nose. Then a sharp voice interrupted her daydreams.

"Stop right where you are, or I'll drop you where you stand."

Chapter Three

All of Liam's senses ramped up to high alert but instead of charging from beneath the bleachers to defend Katie like he wanted to, he flattened his body against the metal bars that crisscrossed his hiding place. He wouldn't be doing either one of them any favors by rushing out to protect her. Besides, a Tempest security guard wouldn't shoot an employee in cold blood...would he?

He peered through the bars, his heart hammering against his chest at the sight of Katie with her arms in the air, a weapon pointed at her back.

A woman's voice cut through the air. "Meyers, put down that gun."

The security guard lowered his weapon as he stammered. "I—I—I'm sorry, Ms. Spann, but civilian employees aren't supposed to be out here on the track."

Ginger Spann waved her long fingers in the air. "The infraction of that rule is certainly not punishable by death. Turn around, dear."

Katie turned to face the duo, and Liam had to give her credit. She didn't shift her gaze once in his direction, although she had to know he was still ensconced beneath the bleachers.

He couldn't see her expression since the security guard

was now blocking her face, but he could feel ice coming off her in waves, making the chilly air even crisper.

"What is going on? I come outside to eat my lunch in the fresh air and I'm held at gunpoint?" She shook her empty sandwich bag, which she'd pulled from her pocket, in the security guard's face.

"I agree, KC." Ginger tilted her head to one side. "It is KC, isn't it? Down in programming?"

Katie worked in programming? That made total sense... and could be useful.

"That's right, and you're Ginger Spann. I just saw you at the all-hands meeting."

"So sad about Garrett Patterson. Maybe that's why we're all on edge." She turned to the security guard. "Meyers, apologize to Ms. Locke."

Meyers shifted from one foot to the other. "I'm sorry, ma'am. It's just that we have strict orders about this area of the—"

"That's enough, Meyers. You can return to whatever it was you were doing before you scared the wits out of Ms. Locke."

"Yes, ma'am." Meyers spun around, and Liam caught a glimpse of the man's tight mouth as he walked toward the gym.

Seems he didn't care much for Ginger's tone, but then, who did?

His departure gave Liam a clear view of Katie's face.

Her wind-tossed, dark hair blew across her face, and she scooped it into a ponytail, holding it over one shoulder. "I'm really sorry about venturing this far. After the news about Garrett, I just wanted to get out of the building for lunch and get some fresh air. I wasn't paying any attention to where I was going, and when I looked up I realized I was way out here, so I just sat on the bleachers to eat my sandwich."

Ginger raised her suit-clad shoulders. "No harm, no foul. It's just that we have training going on out here for potential agents. You knew that, right? Everyone knows that, I suppose."

"That's the buzz, anyway."

The wind gusted, and Ginger tugged at the lapels of her suit jacket.

She wasn't dressed for a turn around the track in this weather. Had the security guard spotted Katie first before calling Ginger? If so, had he seen her emerge from beneath the bleachers?

"It's chilly out here. Let's walk back together."

Liam twisted his lips. That was a less-than-subtle way to get Katie out of this area.

As the two women turned and took the path back to the office buildings, Liam let out a long breath.

What was Katie doing working for Tempest in what amounted to an undercover situation? That was *his* job.

If she was here in a legitimate position as a programmer, why would she come on under an assumed name? She'd called herself KC when she was a teenager in foster care, had switched to the more formal Kathryn when she became an adult and started working and then settled on Katie, which suited her a lot better than Kathryn or KC.

Now she was KC again.

KC was the wild child, the rebel, the illegal hacker, even though she dressed like an office drone. Did calling herself KC have some significance here?

He narrowed his eyes and peered between the bleachers at the empty track. He'd skipped lunch to run a few miles, so he'd better work up a sweat to bolster his story.

He slipped between the slats and hoisted himself on top of the bleachers. Lifting his knees almost to his chest, he began running the stairs. A few trips up and back and sweat dampened his gray T-shirt and beaded his brow.

As he slung his towel around his neck, he peered at the office buildings in the distance. What kind of game was Katie playing with Tempest?

She had to know that if she lost even one round of that game, it could mean her life.

KATIE TOOK A deep breath and hunched over the sink in the bathroom. For a minute she thought Ginger was going to follow her in here. The woman gave her the creeps, and that had been before she'd watched her kill a man in cold blood in midcoitus.

Ginger had shown a lot of interest in Katie's work. Had asked her several questions about programming and what programming languages she knew.

Katie splashed some cold water on her face even though her cheeks still stung from the crisp air outside.

She blotted her face with a paper towel and then crumpled it in her fist. Ginger had no reason to suspect her. Neither she nor the security guard had seen Liam crouching beneath the bleachers.

Meyers—had he been the same guy who'd assisted Ginger last night? He'd been wearing black gloves so if he did have the bird tattoo, she couldn't see it. The voice sounded similar and besides, how many guards did Ginger have that would willingly be an accomplice to murder?

She tossed the paper towel in the trash and straightened her shoulders. Ginger didn't scare her. She still planned to gather more evidence against Tempest and then report the agency to…someone. She hadn't gotten that far in her plan yet.

Her head swiveled back toward the mirror, and she ran her hands through her wind-tossed hair. She'd thought Liam McCabe was the kind of man to turn to in dire straits, but not if he was working with the enemy.

Or was he?

Sebastian certainly hadn't known what he was getting himself into.

She pushed out of the ladies' room and turned the corner to catch the elevator down to her floor. The phone rang just as she stepped into her cubicle, and she spent fifteen minutes dealing with a software issue.

"Where did you disappear to for lunch?" Samantha hung on the corner of her cube.

"I wandered around outside for a bit. How was your meeting?"

Samantha rolled her eyes. "A huge waste of time, and Larry didn't even buy me lunch, the cheap bastard."

"That's just wrong."

"Cute jacket." Samantha tilted her head. "Do you have the sweater you borrowed from me yesterday?"

"Oh, yeah. It's hanging in the closet." Katie jerked her thumb at the metal black cabinet behind her that had a bar and a couple of hangers.

Samantha reached past her and opened the door. She shook out the cream-colored sweater she usually kept on the back of her chair for the days when the office got too chilly—like today.

"I hope you sew."

"What?" Katie clicked on an email reminding her about database maintenance tomorrow night and then deleted it.

"There's a button missing, and I swear it wasn't missing when I gave the sweater to you yesterday."

Katie spun around in her chair. "Really?"

Samantha thrust the sweater at her and a few scraggly threads marked the spot where a square button had been.

"I'm so sorry. Do you have a replacement for it? I can sew it back on."

Samantha laughed. "I'm just kidding. I might have an extra button for this old thing at home. I'll sew it back on when I find it."

"I'll check my car. I didn't bring it in to my place last night. I wore it to my car and tossed it in the backseat so I wouldn't forget it today."

"Don't knock yourself out." She draped the sweater over her shoulders. "It's just my office sweater. I wouldn't actually go out in public wearing this thing."

"The buttons are kind of cute."

"These?" She plucked at one of the shiny squares. "They're hideous."

Samantha retreated to her own cubicle, and Katie dug into her work. She hadn't figured out a way around the Tempest firewalls yet, but she would. She'd been something of a hacker before she went legitimate, and while changing a few grades didn't compare to the type of security Tempest had in place, she had confidence in her skills. She'd already figured out how to mess with the security cameras and the access cards.

She stretched and wandered to the window, folding her arms as she rested her forehead against the glass. She couldn't quite see the track from here, but she could see the edge of the gym, and the movement over there meant the agents were training again.

She knew they slept here. They had living quarters behind the compound out there. Some of them wouldn't make the cut, and they'd be sent home after signing some nondisclosure agreement. They agreed not to talk about their training, and they walked away with a nice severance bonus—at least that's what she'd heard.

She had no doubt Liam would pass every physical test they threw at him. When she'd met him in San Diego, he'd been a SEAL—conditioned, primed and at his peak.

From the looks of him today in his T-shirt and running shorts, he was still at his peak. She chewed on her bottom lip. Maybe she should warn him. But warn him about what? She had no idea really what Tempest was up to. She just knew it was no good, and maybe Liam knew that, too.

She couldn't believe he'd turn on her, but then she wouldn't have believed he'd leave her stranded, high and dry in San Diego, while he returned to the Middle East for another tour. He'd promised her he was done.

She snorted and squiggled her finger through the mist her breath had left on the window. Men like Liam were never done. Men like Sebastian.

She needed another break. She dipped back into her cubicle and dragged her car keys from her purse. Tapping on the side of Samantha's cubicle, she said, "I'm going out to my car in case anyone's looking for me. I'm going to look for that button."

"I don't care about the stupid button, KC."

"I know, but it's bugging me now, and I need a break, anyway."

"If you remember, get me a diet cola from the vending machine downstairs. I'm gonna need some caffeine if I'm gonna get through this boring stuff before I leave tonight."

Katie patted the pocket of her jacket where she had a few dollar bills. "No problem."

She made her way to the parking structure, where cars still took up the majority of the spaces. Most of the employees took off around five o'clock, except for the diehards, people like Ginger and Garrett and Mr. Romo. Nobody ever saw much of Mr. Romo, and nobody ever called him anything but Mr. Romo, but he presided over Tempest from the top floor of the building like some omniscient being. She'd caught sight of him a few times, and he always seemed to be staring at her, but that was probably because he had the oddest, light-colored eyes.

Katie had her doubts he ever left the compound.

She clicked her remote, and her horn beeped once. She went straight for the backseat, running her palms along the leather. Then she lay on her stomach and scanned the floor for the shiny button. She even slipped her hands between the seat cushions.

Her fingertips skimmed the edge of a long-lost nickel. She pulled it free and tucked it into the pocket of her slacks.

Blowing a wisp of hair from her face, she shimmied out of the backseat and slid behind the wheel of the car. She scooped a fistful of quarters from the cup holder to make sure she had enough money for Samantha's soda and one for herself.

Then she tilted her head back against the headrest. When had she lost that button? She hadn't been too many places after borrowing the sweater from Sam at the end of the workday.

She'd worked late in her cubicle after everyone had left to give herself time to do her weekly roaming of the hallways. She'd finally lucked out when she discovered Garrett Patterson's door unlocked—at least she'd considered herself lucky until Ginger had murdered Garrett.

Could she have lost the button hiding in that closet?

Or was it worse than that? She pressed her fingertips to her lips as she recalled the sweater getting caught on Garrett's chair as she wiped her prints from his desk.

No point in returning to his office even if she could get in. If she'd lost the button there, it was either hidden or someone had found it and disposed of it. A button was a button, and it could've come from anywhere.

She scooted from the car and deposited the rest of the change into her pocket. She slammed the car door and leaned forward to peer at her reflection. This dry weather wasn't doing her hair any favors—not that she had cared about her appearance here at Tempest one iota until Liam had shown up on the scene. The man still caused her blood to simmer despite her resolve not to let him affect her. She couldn't afford the distraction.

A movement reflected in the glass caught her eye, and she spun around. The blank headlights on the rows of cars parked in their orderly places stared back at her.

She cocked her head, listening for the beep of a remote or the slamming of a car door. Her own heavy breathing answered her.

Maybe someone had just come back to his car to get something or take a break. Nobody at Tempest had any reason to suspect her of snooping. Sure, Ginger and Meyers had caught her near the track, but she wouldn't be the first female employee at Tempest to try to get a better look at the buff recruits as they went through their paces.

Wiping her palms on her slacks, she strode toward the parking structure's elevator and jabbed the button. When the doors closed, she released a sigh and sagged against the wall of the elevator.

It had been a long time since she'd practiced this cloak-and-dagger stuff. She'd stopped hacking shortly after turning eighteen. Sergeant Liz Humphries, the cop who'd taken an interest in Katie while she'd still been in the foster care system, had undertaken the chore of teaching her right from wrong and more important at the time, the difference between a juvenile record and an adult record.

The same woman had encouraged a rebellious Sebastian to enlist in the Marine Corps. Liz had been a surrogate mother to both of them, creating an unbreakable bond between them at the same time—unbreakable until Sebastian's death.

She blinked back tears as she crossed the courtyard between the parking garage and the office building. As soon as she had proof that Tempest was responsible for Sebastian's death, she'd blow this organization sky-high. And if Liam was still with Tempest, she'd blow him sky high with it.

She swung by the lunchroom and fed her dollar bills

and coins into the soda machine. With a can in each hand, she returned to her office on the first floor. She swiped her card and sailed through the free-standing desks at the front of the office toward the cubicles in the back of the room.

She leaned into Samantha's empty cubicle and placed the can on the edge of her desk in the only spot not covered with papers.

Something gleamed under the lamp on Samantha's desk blotter, and Katie reached out and smoothed her fingers along the edges of the square button.

She blew out a breath. Samantha must've found it in the office. Maybe it had fallen off the sweater in her cube before Katie had even borrowed it.

She returned to her own cubicle and popped the tab on her soda. She had one bug fix to take care of, and then she planned to do a little digging into Liam's file if she could get in there. She'd hacked into other recruits' files but had never found Sebastian's. Of course, Sebastian had been a full-fledged Tempest agent and not just a recruit. She hadn't discovered that database yet.

She laced her fingers and cracked her knuckles over her keyboard. "Just give me time."

A gust of Samantha's flowery perfume announced her presence. "Thanks for the soda."

"You're welcome. I see you have the button. If you want, I'll sew it on for you."

Samantha held up her hands, wiggling her fingers, topped with long, blue fingernails. "Despite these nails, I'm rather handy with a needle. Don't worry about it."

"Where'd you find it? I bet it was in your cube all along. It had probably come off even before you loaned the sweater to me."

"No, it didn't." Samantha put her lips to the can and took a sip. "Someone found it and returned it to me."

"Really?" Katie's hands hovered over her keyboard. "Someone actually found a button and knew it was yours?"

"Said he'd noticed the sweater on me before because his sister had one like it." She shrugged. "Maybe he'd been checking me out."

"He?" Katie dropped her hands to her lap, threading her fingers together so tightly the knuckles turned white.

"One of the security guards."

A muscle ticked in Katie's jaw. "Which one?"

"The big guy with the tattoo of a bird on his hand—Meyers."

Chapter Four

Katie took a quick swig of her soda, and the carbonation fizzed against the back of her throat, making her eyes water. "Where'd he find it?"

"Outside the ladies' room."

"That's just weird that he knew it belonged to you."

"I don't know. The buttons are kind of distinctive—ugly but distinctive. Like I said, he said his sister had one like it. Whatever, I got the button back and you're off the hook." She raised her can and disappeared into her own work area.

Katie closed her eyes and wrapped her hands around the sweating can. Meyers had a tattoo of a bird. He'd been the one helping Ginger in Patterson's office and the one who had held her at gunpoint on the track. Now he'd found Samantha's button.

Was he pulling for employee of the month?

Pressing her damp fingers against her cheeks, she let out a long breath. So, Meyers found the button outside the ladies' room, recognized it as Samantha's and returned it to her. Nothing odd about that. He'd notice an attractive blonde like Sam, had probably been checking her out and maybe thought this was his chance to talk to her.

If he had found the button in Garrett's office, would he really run around the company trying to find its owner? Would they be that obvious?

Her computer blipped and an instant message popped up in the lower right-hand corner of her screen.

What r u really doing at Tempest?

A trickle of fear crept down her spine. The usual name that accompanied an instant message read *user*. This could be anyone testing her. Someone had seen her with Liam at the track.

She typed where the blinking cursor invited.

Who is this?

You have a tattoo of a mermaid just above your right pelvic bone.

Even sitting at her desk, she squirmed at Liam's reference to her tattoo. The man had gotten to know her body very well during their time together in San Diego.

She typed her response.

R u going to rat me out?

Same stairwell at 8 tonight.

What choice did she have? If she refused to meet him, he just might let her real name drop, and then Tempest would make the connection between her and Sebastian. KC Locke had no history with Sebastian Cole, but Katie O'Keefe did. She'd worked too hard to scrub her background and identity. She didn't need Liam McCabe to come along and blow it all up.

Not that she really believed Liam would expose her. Even if Liam knew her true purpose here, he'd never do anything to harm her. Although he'd bruised her heart, he'd move heaven and earth to protect her, and she'd do the same by telling him to run as far away from Tempest as he could.

The rest of the afternoon flew by with her joint efforts at doing her real job and continuing her assault on the firewalls Tempest had set up. Whoever had put them in place was damned good.

She jerked her head up and blinked her eyes when Samantha banged on the side of her cubicle. "Whoa, take it easy."

"I've been saying your name and tapping on the edge of your cube for the past minute. It's quittin' time, girl. A few of us are going to the Deluxe Bar for a couple of cocktails. Do you want to join us?"

"I'll pass. I have a problem to work through, so I'm going to stick around until I figure it out."

Samantha saluted. "Now that's what I call dedication. If you figure it out quickly, join us. We'll be there for a few hours."

"Will do. Have fun."

When Samantha left at five-twenty, Katie got a bag of chips from the vending machine and returned to her desk, slumping in her chair as she ripped open the bag.

"Are you working late?"

She glanced up, and her heart skipped a beat as Meyers's form filled the opening to her cubicle, his two hands wedged on either side of the edges as if blocking her exit.

She swallowed her chip and wiped her greasy fingers on a tissue. "I can get more work done when it's quiet."

"I just wanted to apologize for this afternoon. Management keeps us on our toes about protecting that area where the recruits are housed."

"I understand."

"We're kind of damned if we do, damned if we don't.

We're supposed to keep a close eye on it, but then we get in trouble for overreacting."

"Didn't mean to get you in trouble. I'll be more careful where I wander around next time."

"Yeah, just, sorry."

"Me, too."

He scratched the heavy stubble on his chin, causing the bird on his hand to move its wings. "Samantha leave for the day?"

"Uh-huh." She stuffed another chip in her mouth to end the conversation.

"Does she have a boyfriend?" He stared at his thumb while picking at his cuticle.

Her tense shoulders dropped. So, he had a thing for Samantha and probably *did* know the button he'd found belonged to her and used it as an excuse to talk to her.

"Nope." Not that she wanted to give Meyers false hope, but he wasn't Sam's type, anyway, and after his complicity in Patterson's death last night, she sure as hell wouldn't let Samantha date him.

"She likes those recruits, huh?"

Her spine stiffened again. He sure was keeping tabs on Samantha. "Oh, I wouldn't say that, no more than any other woman around here."

"I'll let you get back to work. Just wanted to apologize for drawing my gun on you this afternoon."

"Thanks." She swiveled her chair in front of her keyboard and popped another chip into her mouth, listening for the office door to close behind Meyers.

She worked for a few more hours, glancing at the time on her computer every ten minutes, not able to concentrate on anything. She'd never get through Tempest's firewalls with her mind on Liam.

At ten minutes to eight, she scrubbed the history on her computer, including her instant messages. Then she logged off and snatched her access card from the card reader on her computer. She had a date in a stairwell.

She headed for the elevator like she did every night, but when she got off at the second floor, she entered the stairwell instead of heading to the exit for the parking garage. She jogged up two flights of stairs and ducked beneath the staircase.

A door above her scraped open, and she held her breath until Liam came into view.

He joined her, huddling so close she could smell the fresh scent of his soap and the mint of his toothpaste. He placed his lips close to her ear. "Did you get rid of those instant messages we traded?"

"Of course. I should be asking you that."

"I had a good teacher show me how to cover my tracks on a computer." He touched his finger to her nose.

She jerked her head and he dropped his hand. "Would you really blow my cover?"

"To keep you safe and get you away from Tempest? Maybe."

She caught her breath. Did he realize the danger at Tempest, or was this some kind of trick?

"What are you talking about? We both work for Tempest."

"Under somewhat assumed identities."

"Are you telling me they don't know you're Liam McCabe, former navy SEAL and all-around badass?" She narrowed her eyes.

"I like that description. Maybe I'll put it on my next business card."

She punched his arm, her fist meeting rock-solid muscle. "Be serious."

"They know I'm Liam McCabe, former navy SEAL, and they know about my badassery." He raised an eyebrow. "But that's where my identity ends as far as Tempest is concerned."

"What does that mean? What else is there?"

"What happened last night in Patterson's office? Why were you up here?"

She sighed. Maybe if she started answering some of his questions, he'd start answering some of hers.

"I've been searching Tempest at night, trying to find unlocked offices, looking for evidence. Patterson had left his office unlocked last night, and I slipped inside."

Liam pressed the heel of his hand against his forehead. "And you found him dead?"

"Worse than that. He came into the office while I was there, and I had to hide in the closet. Ginger Spann followed him, and...and she murdered him."

His body stiffened. "Are you sure? How?"

"She injected him with something that mimicked a heart attack. I heard the whole thing, Liam. Then she got some security guard in there to help her—the same security guard who pulled a gun on me at the track."

"They didn't see you?"

"No."

He took her by the shoulders and squeezed. "Why are you doing this, Katie? What's Tempest to you? And I want the truth. Tempest isn't some high school or hapless government agency that you can hack into for fun and games."

Staring into Liam's blue eyes, she felt safe for the first time since arriving at Tempest. He didn't seem that surprised about the murder, and he was obviously hiding something from Tempest. She could trust him. She could always trust Liam, except when it came to staying by her side.

She closed her eyes and let out a shuddering breath. "It's Sebastian."

"Sebastian? You told me he was dead."

"He is—and Tempest killed him."

"What? How? You have proof of this?"

"One question at a time." She placed her hands against his chest, and his heart thundered beneath her palm.

"He killed himself, Liam." Her nose stung, and she sniffled back the tears.

Liam's touch on her shoulders turned into a caress, and he pulled her snug against his body. "I'm so sorry, Katie. Was it the drugs again?"

She wrenched away from him. "Absolutely not. He'd been clean and sober for years. It was Tempest."

"You keep saying that, but how was Tempest responsible for his suicide?"

"They recruited him to be an agent—just like you—and after he'd made the grade and had worked for them for just over a year, he killed himself."

Her words slammed against his brain, and he blinked to clear the fog. Sebastian Cole was the Tempest agent who'd killed himself? He'd known about the agent but didn't know his name…until now. He didn't want to color Katie's perceptions or lead her on, so he kept his tone as neutral as he could.

"Why are you laying his suicide at Tempest's gates?"

She threw up her hands and took a half turn in the small space. "Because I saw him before and after. He was in a good place. He was thrilled Tempest wanted him. While he was in the marines, he'd heard rumors about the covert agencies and how much good they accomplished under the radar."

Liam pressed his lips into a thin line. As a SEAL he'd heard the rumors, too, but it was Prospero, not Tempest, who ruled the shadow operations. Tempest had always been second best, and then the agency had turned to the dark side, but no one knew to what extent.

"Then what? He came here?"

She nodded. "Yes, he came here as a recruit. I saw him once after he completed the training and already there was something off about him, but he seemed happy so I was happy."

A pulse danced in his jaw and he rubbed it into submission. Did Tempest start in with the recruits while they were still in training? "What was off about him?"

"He seemed a little detached, distant. I chalked it up to the covert nature of his training and work." She fluttered her lashes. "R-reminded me of you when you first got back from a mission."

Great. If she'd thought him detached and distant when he'd been a SEAL, what would she think of him as a covert ops agent?

"You saw him again?"

"It was worse the next time, the last time I saw him." Her bottom lip trembled, and he wanted to kiss away her pain. "He was angry, cold, closed up. He pushed me away."

God, just like he'd done when he'd decided to do another tour of duty while she'd been busy planning a life with him. Katie-O deserved so much more. This fearless woman at least deserved the truth.

He looked her straight in the eyes. "And then he shot himself in France while he was on an assignment."

Her mouth dropped open, and she took a step back. "How do you know that?"

"That's what I'm doing here, Katie."

"You're here because of Sebastian's death?"

"Partly."

Crossing her arms across her chest, she tilted her head to one side. "You're not a navy SEAL anymore, are you?"

"I'm working for another covert agency."

She snorted before he could finish. "That's swell. So you're over here, what? Stealing their secrets to success?"

"Katie." He grabbed her fidgeting hands. "Tempest is

bad news. It's not just Sebastian's suicide we're investigating, and no, I didn't realize the dead agent was Sebastian Cole. Another Tempest agent went on a rampage and had to be stopped. Another agent is on the run."

"What is Tempest doing to them? What's going on?"

"Drugs, brainwashing, mind control."

"I suspected as much." She sagged against him. "Why? What's their goal?"

"Their overall goal? We're not sure yet, but their goal for the agents is just that—mind control."

"To turn them into robots that'll do whatever they're told, no matter how unscrupulous." Her dark eyes widened. "That's what Sebastian was, some kind of robot."

Tears streamed silently down her cheeks, and she did nothing to stop them or wipe them away.

He cupped her face with his hands and smoothed his thumbs across the wet trails on her flushed skin. "I'm sorry, Katie. I know how much Sebastian meant to you."

Her body jerked, and she grabbed two handfuls of his jacket. "And what are you? Some kind of canary in the coal mine? If your…agency already knows what Tempest is doing to its agents, why do you need to be here to experience it firsthand?"

"We know what Tempest is doing, but we don't exactly know how, and we don't know when it all starts. It was important for someone to infiltrate the compound."

"Why does it have to be you?" Her voice rose, almost on a wail. "Why does it always have to be you?"

He put two fingers to her soft lips. "Shh. It's going to be okay. What's not okay is your presence here. You need to quit and leave as soon as possible."

"You need me." She wiped her sleeve across her nose. "I'm getting close to hacking through Tempest's firewalls. When I do, I can bring them down financially. I can hit them where it hurts. I'll make them pay for what they did to Sebastian."

The fire in Katie's eyes practically lit up the dim stairwell, and a thrill zapped his body. This was exactly why he'd fallen in love with this woman, exactly why she terrified him.

He pressed his lips to her hot forehead. "The computer stuff would be great but not necessary right now, not worth your safety."

"I am safe. I went through a lot of trouble to get this gig, and I'm not giving it up—for anyone. Did you give up your job for me?"

A flash of heat claimed his chest and crawled up his neck. He hadn't. He'd done what he believed was his last mission for his SEAL team, was ready to settle down with Katie when he got the call. They'd needed him, needed him more than Katie with her prickly, standoffish attitude.

"No, I didn't."

"Exactly." She pushed the hair from her face, pushing his hands away at the same time. "I have a job to do here. I have to avenge Sebastian's death, and I'm gonna do it with or without you."

How the hell could anyone resist a woman like Katie?

"Then we work together. You keep me posted and I'll keep—"

Katie grabbed his wrist and dug her fingernails into his flesh, while pointing at the ceiling.

Then he heard it—someone jiggling the handle on the metal door on the floor above. Good thing he'd rigged it.

Katie dragged at his arm and whispered. "We need to get out of here."

"He won't be able to get in for several minutes because I jammed the door. Let's go downstairs."

Placing his hand on the small of Katie's back, he propelled her down the stairs ahead of him. They passed the third floor and headed to the second, which was on the same level as the bridge to the parking garage.

He jerked his thumb at the door.

She shook her head and pointed down. Then she leaned in close, her hair tickling his chin, and whispered, "I have to do some cleanup on the security camera footage and my access badge."

Katie had a brain that wouldn't quit and a body to match.

"What time are you leaving? It's probably not safe in that parking structure after hours."

"Are you kidding? Nobody can get on and off this compound with the tight security Tempest has. Only employees are allowed in the parking structure."

"That's what worries me."

They jogged down one more flight. Placing his hands against the metal door, he cocked his head and listened. He inched the door open and peered through the resulting crack. All clear.

He grabbed Katie around the waist and turned her toward him. "Be careful. This ain't no video game, Katie. This is life and death."

"I know that." She touched his face with her fingertips. "Don't let them do anything to you, Liam. Don't let them change you."

"Don't worry." And then he did something he'd been dreaming about for the past two years. He kissed Katie O'Keefe, intrepid sleuth, hacker extraordinaire, woman of his dreams, on the mouth.

Chapter Five

Katie slipped back up to her cubicle and dropped to her chair, her fingers pressed to her buzzing lips. Even a quick, hard kiss in a cold stairwell from Liam McCabe beat any other lip-lock she'd experienced in the past few years.

She squared her shoulders and stuck her card into the card reader on her computer. The kiss didn't mean anything—just his way of sealing the deal that they'd work together on this thing. She didn't want to jump back into a relationship with Liam, anyway. She had life-and-death matters to take care of now.

She logged on to her computer, and her fingers flew across the keyboard. She'd broken into the security cameras weeks ago, which allowed her to freeze the cameras and erase certain inconvenient images. That capability allowed her to wander around the facility at night, as long as she stayed a few steps ahead of security.

Would security make anything of the jammed door? Given the high level of paranoia around here, most likely. She and Liam would probably have to find another secure meeting place. She'd check out the online map of the buildings and the surrounding area to look for something.

Once she adjusted the footage from the security cameras, she got into the access badge area, located her badge code and erased the recorded swipes of her leaving and entering her office area. If the rigged stairwell door sent someone on a quest to identify late workers and trace their movements, she'd be safe. According to the computer codes, she'd never left her office.

Liam didn't seem to have an access badge, so how he managed to wander around the compound at night, she didn't have a clue. But Liam could do just about anything he put his mind to, and the thought of working with him excited her.

She wrapped up her work and headed to the parking garage. As she strode across the quad to the structure, her nose twitched at the smell of a cigarette. Her steps slowed as she picked out two figures lurking near the entrance to the garage and a pinpoint of light glowing in the dark.

Tensing her muscles, she drew closer, and one of the men turned his head in profile. She instantly recognized Liam. He'd been worried about her leaving late, but who was smoking the cigarette next to him?

She cleared her throat and clutched her purse under her arm.

The cigarette smoker spoke first. "It's okay, ma'am. It's just us recruits from across campus."

"Oh, I was wondering who was out here so late." She pointed at the cigarette, ignoring Liam. "I don't think smoking is allowed on the facility grounds."

The man threw back his head and laughed. "If it's not even allowed on the facility grounds, can you imagine the consequences if the powers-that-be found out a recruit was smoking?"

"Is that what you two are doing over here? Sneaking smokes?"

He crushed the cigarette against the side of the parking structure. "Kinda like middle school, huh? That's what I'm doing out here, anyway. I'm Dustin, by the way, and this is Liam, and I don't know what the hell he was doing here."

"I'm KC, and I really don't think we're supposed to be fraternizing."

Dustin snorted. "You mean like the school dance in the gym? The employees stand on one side and the recruits stand on the other like a bunch of wallflowers? Just like middle school."

He held up the butt of his extinguished cigarette. "You won't tell the principal, will you? Principal Romo, or worse yet, Vice Principal Spann?"

She shrugged her shoulders, made stiff by Dustin and his irreverent comments. Was he trying to trap her? Trap Liam?

Liam had obviously been lurking around the parking garage to keep an eye on her as she left the property, and Dustin had discovered him. Or had he followed him?

"Whatever you do is your business."

He held out the butt. "You wanna take this with you? Destroy the evidence? Help a brother out?"

She folded her arms, tucking her hands beneath her armpits. "I—I..."

"Let's go, man." Liam took the cigarette from Dustin's fingers and plowed his toe into the loose rocks on the ground. He dropped the butt onto the rocks and with his boot, covered it with more rocks. "We have a long day ahead of us tomorrow, and you still need to rinse that tobacco smell out of your mouth."

"Okay, okay." Dustin held up his hands in surrender. "I'm just messin' with you, KC. If you don't rat me out, I won't rat you out."

She forced a laugh and regretted the fake tone. "I won't rat you out, but all I'm doing is leaving work after a long day."

"If you say so." Dustin's eyes shifted from her to Liam.

Liam nudged Dustin's arm. "Let's get back before lights out."

As she passed them, Liam said, "Have a nice evening, ma'am."

She put her head down and scurried to her car, looking neither right nor left. She didn't want to run into anyone else.

Liam had taken a big risk hanging around to see her off. Was Dustin even a smoker or was it all a ploy to get them in his confidence? She had no intention of playing that game.

She trusted no one here—no one except Liam.

As soon as she dropped onto the seat of her car and closed the door, she sank against the backrest and relaxed her muscles. She had to pick up the pace on her efforts to hack through Tempest's computer system. She couldn't take much more of this stress. She'd much rather be in San Diego with her chocolate lab, Mario, working on the newest video game.

Of course, Liam's appearance on the scene and knowing they were on the same team had just brightened the situation considerably.

She'd have to show him some pictures of Mario. They'd been looking for a dog together before he'd up and decided to abandon her. And then in the dark days after Liam had left, Mario had found her. They'd found each other. Figured one lost soul would seek out another.

God, she missed that little guy.

She sighed and cranked on the engine. Her tires squealed on the cement as she wound her way down the parking structure. She followed the long road out toward the guard shack and waved to the attendant on duty as he raised the parking arm for her.

Tempest's facility was located about five miles from a small town on one of the many lakes up here. The residential area, where most of the Tempest employees lived, fanned out from the town with the more expensive homes farther afield and situated at the lake's edge. Tempest employees, retirees and ski resort workers populated the town and environs since the logging company had closed down several years ago.

As she sped down the highway, she glanced at the illuminated numbers on her dashboard clock. It had been over three hours since Samantha had left the office. She and the others had probably deserted the Deluxe by now. Thankfully, she still had a half a bottle of wine in her fridge. After the day she had, she could use a glass or two. She needed two just to turn off her brain.

She took the turnoff for the town, anyway, and rolled through the quiet streets. A couple of cars were parked in front of the bar—not enough to make it worth her while.

She swung out of town and hit the highway again. She lived in an apartment complex peopled with a few Tempest employees and a gaggle of retirees from California—more functional than fancy, but private.

A set of taillights up ahead had her tapping her brakes. Traffic often clogged this road, the only one into and out of town, but not usually at this time of night. As she crested the hill behind two other cars, a flood of lights illuminated the night sky.

Red-and-orange emergency lights revolved, looking almost festive. The cars ahead of her blocked her view of the accident, and she slowed to a crawl as the cops directed single-file traffic to the left.

She drew abreast of the scene and rubber-necked just like everyone else. A single car sat smashed and battered at the side of the road. Looked like a tow truck had dragged it up from the ravine.

As she inched past, she shivered at the back window with cracks running from one side to the other. Then her heart stopped and she slammed on her brakes. The car behind her honked, but she barely noticed.

A large, yellow O on the back of the windshield had caught her attention. Samantha had gone to the University of Oregon and had proudly displayed her alma mater's sticker on the back of her blue sedan. Was that car blue? She couldn't tell in the lights.

She swerved to the right, just ahead of the accident scene and threw her car into Park. She scrambled from the car, flinging out her arms to catch her balance. Her heels crunched against the gravel as she made her way toward the crumpled car.

A police officer stopped her progress. "Hold on, miss. You need to stay back."

"I think I know that car. Is it a woman? Is she okay?"

"It was a woman, but I can't tell you any more, miss. You'll have to get back in your car and move along."

Standing on her tiptoes, she peered over his shoulder, her heart pounding a mile a minute. "Is it a blue sedan? Was a blonde driving the car? Is she okay?"

"Miss—" he spread his arms out "—you're going to have to move along now."

"Okay, okay." She plowed a hand through her hair, her gaze shifting across the street. If she dashed across the highway, she could sneak around the perimeter the back way.

She spun around and walked back to her car. When the cop's attention had returned to directing traffic, she scurried across the road, dodging between the creeping cars all slowing down to get a better look.

She stumbled back down the highway on the other side of the street. Once clear of the accident scene, she ran back across the road.

She slipped past a tow truck driver and zeroed in on the crippled car. Her knees weakened as she recognized Samantha's blue sedan. Her gaze tracked to the stretcher beside the ambulance. An EMT was securing a strap around a form tucked beneath a white sheet.

In a daze she walked toward the stretcher, shaking off someone's grasp. When she reached the side of the stretcher, she saw silky locks of blond hair, streaked with blood, hanging over the side.

She gulped for a breath but it wasn't enough. The night grew darker around her, and she sank to her knees.

Chapter Six

Liam held his plate of egg whites in one hand as he scanned the cafeteria. Dustin was right. This was all reminiscent of middle school, and he'd better go sit with the popular kids so he wouldn't be an outcast. He didn't want to appear different, and he didn't want Dustin to think he was avoiding him because he'd discovered him hanging around the employee parking structure last night.

He pulled out a chair, and his plate clattered as he set it on the table. He nodded to the other men and stabbed a clump of scrambled egg with his fork.

Dustin eyed him over the rim of his coffee cup. "Did you hear the news?"

Swallowing, he shook his head. "Did they up the number of pull-ups on us?"

Charlie, sitting next to Dustin, flexed his biceps. "Let 'em try. I'm ready."

Dustin rolled his eyes. "Another Tempest employee bit the dust."

Liam almost choked on the orange juice going down his throat and managed to turn it into a cough. "Really? Another heart attack? Maybe the stress of working here is getting to the civilians."

"It was an accident out on highway 26—a woman."

Liam wanted to jump up and throttle Dustin to get him

to talk faster, but he felt the other man's dark eyes on him, studying him. "That's too bad. Single car or were there more people involved?"

"Single car. She plunged into the ravine off the highway, no seat belt."

Charlie waved his fork in the air. "I heard she'd been drinking at the Deluxe."

Pain throbbed against Liam's temple, and the eggs tasted like chalk in his mouth. He couldn't ask the name of the employee because he really wasn't supposed to know any names, and he couldn't tip his hand in front of Dustin by asking if it was KC.

"That sucks." He shrugged. "I just hope they don't pull us into another all-hands meeting for some announcement."

He wolfed down the rest of his breakfast and traded war stories with Charlie on their way to the classroom. They had geo-political studies this morning—nothing he hadn't already covered as a Prospero agent and with a lot more content thrown in, including the US perspective, which seemed to be missing from Tempest's lessons.

Max Duvall, the agent who'd broken free of Tempest, had told them the agency used foreign operatives as well as Americans. This coursework must've been designed for an international student body.

He took his seat in the classroom and logged on to the computer. Then, using tricks he'd learned from Katie, he switched to an anonymous identity and instant messaged her.

Katie-O, you okay?

The cursor blinked at him, mimicking the pulse ticking in his throat.

No answer. She could be away from her desk. He checked the time. Maybe she started late.

He gave her a few more minutes and had to switch to his own identity for the lessons, but he couldn't concentrate on a damned thing.

Maybe someone had seen them at the track. Maybe she hadn't been able to fix the security cameras. Maybe Dustin had reported them. Any number of things could've gone wrong, and they all marched through his brain, pounding against his skull.

He wished Tempest would have another of those gatherings to let them know what was going on, but this case was different from Garrett Patterson. This so-called accident happened away from the facility.

He tapped a key on his keyboard and nothing happened. The groans around the room told him others were having the same problem with their computers.

Mills, the instructor, rapped on the lectern. "It seems we're having some difficulties with the computers in here. I'm going to make a call to IT. You can take a break until then."

Liam stretched and glanced around the room. He needed more info about that accident last night, but didn't want to show undue interest and didn't want Dustin to overhear him.

He wandered out of the room, following a group of guys on their way to the vending machines. The agents in training could get their sugar fixes there, since the recruit diet banned sugars, fats and high-sodium foods.

He braced his hands against the snack machine, studying the candy bars, his ears attuned to the idle chatter. But they had bigger concerns than an accident involving a civilian.

"I've heard the psych test can get you discharged immediately."

"I'm going in showing my aggressive side. I've heard that's what Tempest wants."

"What about you, McCabe? You worried?"

He cranked his head to the side. "About the psych evaluation this afternoon?"

"As a former SEAL, you've probably already been deconstructed and put back together again, anyway."

"I'm not too worried. Let's face it. If you don't have the psych makeup for this job, then you probably don't want the job."

They grumbled amongst themselves but didn't offer him any opportunity to bring up the accident.

Mills poked his head into the room. "We have someone from IT. Those of you having problems, we need you to log back in to your computers."

Liam punched a button for a chocolate bar and strode out of the lunchroom. He hoped this geek couldn't tell if he'd been accessing the computer as an anonymous user.

When he returned to the room and saw the geek, he tripped to a stop. The relief that surged through his body almost had him dropping to his knees.

Katie, dressed in a pair of navy blue slacks and a white blouse was sitting at a computer in the corner, tapping away at the keyboard. Even though he missed her tight jeans, wild hair and black nail polish that she'd sported when they were together in San Diego, he'd never been so happy to see anyone in his life. She didn't look up when he walked into the room.

Mills said, "Here's another one. His computer's in the last row."

Katie leaned back in the chair, stretching her legs in front of her. "You guys need to restart these computers every day. We do automatic downloads, and if your computers are off, they're not going to get the downloads. Some of the stuff you're running in here is out of date."

Mills shoved his glasses to the top of his head. "Our class time is almost over, and the recruits have physical training next, so we'll just call it a morning."

She pushed back from the chair, her gaze flicking in his direction. "That's probably a good idea, but I need each of the guys who were having problems to stay and log in for me so I can run the updates."

"Yeah, they can be late to PT." Mills counted the computers with the blue screens. "Just three more. Jensen, Chang and McCabe stay behind. The rest of you get ready for PT."

Liam had a feeling Katie would get to his computer last. He could wait for her all day, but he might not like what she had to say. If she'd taken the risk to disrupt the computers in this room for a chance to talk to him, it couldn't be good.

She finished fiddling with Jensen's computer. Mills left as Katie sat down with Kenneth Chang, a man of few words and fewer social graces. He grunted in response to Katie's questions and practically charged out of the room when she finished repairing his computer. A guy like that would pass Tempest's psych exam with flying colors.

"Now, let's have a look at yours." She slid into his seat, brought up a document and typed the word *bugged?*

He drew up a chair next to hers. "No. I've been worried sick about you. I heard about the accident, but I couldn't get any more information out of anyone without looking suspicious. Thank God you're okay."

Her fingers trembled as they hovered over the keyboard. "I'm not okay. My friend Samantha Van Alstyn was killed in that crash."

"I'm sorry. I heard there was drinking involved."

She gripped his wrist in a vise. "They killed her because of me."

His heart slammed against his rib cage. "What does that mean?"

"I borrowed Samantha's sweater the day before yester-day. I was wearing it in Patterson's office a-and I think I lost a button by his desk. Meyers, our favorite security guard, returned the button to Samantha."

"So they think Samantha was in that room? Why would they assume she witnessed the murder? She could've lost it there another time."

"Samantha was in accounting. She had no reason to be in Patterson's office."

"If he was putting the moves on Ginger, how do they know he hadn't brought other women to his office?"

"I don't know. You're making these suggestions as if these people are rational beings. They thought there was a chance she was in that office, and they took care of the problem."

He dug his fingers into his left temple. "God, it could've been you."

"How could I be so stupid to leave behind evidence like that button?"

The pain in his head sharpened. "Do they know you and Samantha were friendly? Are they going to think she told you something about Patterson's death?"

"If she told me something about the murder, wouldn't they expect me to hightail it out of here?"

"Maybe, but she didn't leave Tempest and they took care of her, anyway."

"They could've just figured Samantha was seeing Pat-terson but hadn't been in his office during the murder. They got rid of her as a safety measure."

Liam tapped his chin. "Tempest doesn't like loose ends."

The handle of the classroom door turned, and Liam jumped back from Katie and crossed his arms as her eyes widened. "Yeah, it was running a little slow right before the crash."

"You're missing three updates, so I'm going to run those for you right now."

The door eased open, and Dustin poked his head into the room. "Hey, look who's here."

"Yeah, my computer died along with a couple of others." Liam lifted his shoulders.

Putting his finger to his lips, Dustin glanced over his shoulder. "Don't worry. My lips are sealed or I'd have some explaining to do of my own about my nicotine habit."

Liam clenched his jaw. He'd had enough of this guy's veiled threats and innuendos. "Look, man, if you want to tell someone I was walking about the facility last night and got as far as the employee parking garage, knock yourself out."

"Same goes for me. You're the one who started the conversation last night." Katie punched a few more keys.

"I'm just messin' with you." Dustin turned his fingers into a gun and pointed it their way. "Hey, Hamilton sent me to find you, so you can get in a workout before the psychologist starts shrinking our heads."

"Be right out." Liam nodded at his computer. "You need me for anything else?"

"Nope. Just restart your computer, don't forget your access card and have a nice life." Katie gathered her notebook and papers and stuck her pen in the spiral binding of the notebook.

Dustin stepped aside to let her pass, rolling his eyes at Liam.

Liam logged off the computer and snatched his card out of the reader. "Okay, I'm ready to work up a sweat."

After two hours of running, doing sit-ups, push-ups, pull-ups and weight training, Liam returned to his room to shower and get ready for his appointment with one of the docs. Usually a psych eval involved word association, the Rorschach and various situational questions—nothing Prospero hadn't trained him to handle.

Tempest had already run the recruits through this ringer before, thinning their ranks in the process. He didn't know what to expect this time, but Prospero had prepared him for anything.

Since Tempest didn't want the recruits comparing notes, head psychiatrist, Dr. Nealy, herded them into a waiting area with snacks, reading material, DVDs and video games, where they spent the time until their own appointments. Dr. Nealy had a staff of several psychologists to perform multiple evaluations at the same time—a regular assembly line of head-shrinking.

As he entered the holding pen, he nodded to Dustin and Charlie, grabbed an apple and plopped down in one of the beanbag chairs in front of a gaming system. Maybe Katie-O had worked on this game.

The sweater incident and Samantha's death had him re-thinking Katie's role in this investigation. Tempest must be all kinds of paranoid if finding a woman's button in Patterson's office had driven them to murder.

Of course, maybe he and Katie were all kinds of paranoid. Samantha could've drunk too much, gotten into her car and driven off the road all by herself.

The door to the waiting area swung open, and Nealy's assistant called out four names. She hesitated at the door as the recruits filed out of the room. "Remember, gentlemen... and lady, no discussing the evaluations before or after."

Nah, if he had to bet on the paranoia winner, it'd be Tempest.

By the time he'd finished his apple, played a few levels of the video game and leafed through a sports magazine, the assistant was back with another four names—his among them.

He and the other three men followed her into the hallway, where she deposited each of them in an office. At the last door, she turned to him.

"At the end of the session, Dr. Harris will escort you out of her office, and you'll return to your room."

"Why would I do that? Don't we have range this afternoon?"

Her lips formed a tight smile. "I'm sure I don't know, McCabe. Those are the instructions I have."

His pulse jumped. Why would the recruits be going back to their rooms? How long were they expected to be quiet about the evaluations and why?

She opened the door for him, without looking in the room, and he stepped into the dim office. He blinked, taking in the couch against one wall, the chair beside it and the person behind the desk.

She didn't stand as he took another step into the room. Instead, she studied him over the rim of her glasses, like a specimen under a microscope.

This was gonna be fun.

He raised his hand. "I'm Liam McCabe."

"I know who you are. I'm Dr. Harris."

"Where do you want me to sit, Dr. Harris?"

"The couch, please. I'll take the chair."

"Do I have to lie down?" He snorted, but she didn't crack a smile at his attempt to make a joke.

"You can do whatever you like, Liam. You like being in control, don't you?"

She'd jumped right in on the analysis.

He sank into the soft cushion of the couch and crossed an ankle over his knee. "Who doesn't?"

She finally rose from behind her desk, a tall woman whose thin frame made her appear even taller. She pulled the chair closer to the couch and sat, her knees almost touching his.

"But you have to give up some control when you're in the US Military, correct?"

"Sure, yeah, of course, for the greater good of the unit and all that."

She slipped a pencil between two tapered fingers and tapped it on her knee. "You did exhibit a few issues with... excessive violence, didn't you?"

Prospero had planted that little nugget in his file. Tempest seemed to like its agents a little on the outlaw side.

He pinned her with a hard gaze. "It's war. It's violent."

"I get that, Liam. Nobody's judging you here, but I do want to hear more about the incident."

He started reciting the story that Prospero had fed to him. This was his third account of the story, and he stuck to the script. Embellishing could only lead to trouble.

Dr. Harris held up her hand, cutting him off. "That's your conscious remembrance of the event."

"Yeah?" He drew his brows over his nose. What did she have up her sleeve?

She held up her pencil and twirled it slowly between her fingers. "I want to get to the subconscious truth of the incident. I'm going to hypnotize you."

Chapter Seven

Samantha's boss, Larry Turner, hovered at the entrance to Katie's cubicle, his hands shoved into the pockets of his khakis. "I just can't believe it. Sam wasn't even a heavy drinker."

"And if she was so drunk, why'd her so-called friends let her get in the car?"

Larry hunched his shoulders. "I think she left later than they did. One of the guys said she'd been flirting with a stranger."

Katie's stomach dropped, and she folded her arms across her midsection. Had this stranger slipped her something? "D-did the police talk to him?"

"I'm not sure. All I'm hearing is rumor right now." He kicked the empty box at his feet. "I had to talk to her mother today, father's dead. I asked her if she wanted me to pack up Samantha's personal effects and send them to her."

She'd come to realize that Tempest employees shared similar backgrounds—orphans, loners—just like her and Sebastian. "That's not a very pleasant task. Do you want me to help?"

"Funny thing is her mother didn't want Sam's stuff. Said she'd come out later to pack up her apartment but told me I could trash the stuff in her office. Did they have a strained relationship, or what?"

"I have no idea. Samantha never talked about her mother."

"Well, she sounds like a real piece of work to me." Larry nudged the box toward Samantha's cubicle with his foot and ducked inside.

Less than a minute later, he emerged, dangling Samantha's sweater from his fingertips. "Do you want this? You seemed to wear it more than she did."

Katie swallowed. Had other people noticed that, too? She never wanted to see that sweater again as long as she lived.

"No, thanks. I don't think I could wear anything of Samantha's after what happened. In fact, I'm feeling pretty sick to my stomach right now."

"If you worked for me, I'd send you home. You should take off."

"I think I will." She would've gone home if she hadn't been desperate to talk to Liam and tell him about the missing button. It hadn't taken much to incapacitate those computers and to figure out which one belonged to Liam. It had been risky and Dustin had caught them again, but the look on Liam's face when he'd seen her in the classroom had been worth it. Even if he no longer loved her, that look confirmed that he at least cared about her deeply. Or maybe it just meant he didn't want to see her dead.

Okay, that was a start.

"Are you sure you don't need help with Samantha's cubicle?"

"She didn't have much stuff in here. You go home."

She called her boss and logged off. As she walked across the quad to the parking structure, she shaded her eyes and gazed in the direction of the recruits' compound.

At this time of day, you could usually hear the shots from the range. The buildings were soundproof so you had to be outside to hear the gunfire, but she heard nothing from that direction. The recruits had an indoor area for shooting, as well. She should know because she'd worked on some of the computerized scenarios, but usually they split the recruits into outdoor range and indoor training. Not today.

A little flutter of fear winged its way across her chest. The psych exams. Dustin had mentioned something about the psychological testing. Was it starting already? Was Liam safe?

If she lost Liam to these people, too, she'd shut this place down single-handedly if she had to.

She hesitated before punching the button to call the elevator car. Shut the place down? She could do that. She'd incapacitated her entire high school at the end of her junior year just because—computer systems, lights, bell schedule, the works. It had gotten her suspended, but the challenge had given her a thrill. Imagine the thrill of shutting down Tempest?

She stepped into the elevator and as the doors began to close, a large hand slapped the edge. The doors jerked back open, and Meyers stepped into the car.

She clutched her purse and gave him a weak smile.

"Sorry about that. I have to check on that car alarm on the top floor."

"That's okay. Sorry I didn't see you coming."

"Pretty distracted, huh?"

Had he been privy to her daydreams about bringing Tempest operations to a crashing halt? Maybe Tempest read minds, too.

"Umm, yeah."

"I mean about Samantha—terrible accident."

"It was. I just couldn't concentrate, and my boss told me to go home."

"Yeah, I think all the people drinking with her last night stayed home today, too."

"Do you know anything more about what happened than we're hearing from the rumor mill?"

"Probably not. She went out with some coworkers, got behind the wheel when she probably shouldn't have and went into the ravine."

The elevator jostled to a stop at her parking level, and she straddled the door. "Did you hear anything about a guy she met at the Deluxe?"

He raised his eyes to the ceiling. "Didn't hear that but it wouldn't surprise me. Samantha was a pretty girl."

"She was." The doors closed, and she stood staring at the elevator. Car alarm? She didn't hear any car alarm.

Twenty minutes later, she coasted to a stop across the street from the Deluxe Bar. She hadn't planned on coming here, but when she'd passed the off-ramp for the town, she couldn't resist.

The cops who'd investigated the accident scene may have talked to the employees at the Deluxe, but the cops didn't know what she knew about Samantha's employer.

Stepping out of the car, she buttoned her coat. The bar stayed open all day. Just after three o'clock, she had a jump on the happy hour crowd.

She pushed through the front door, and a few heads turned before their owners got back to the serious business of pickling their livers. With the stools on either ends of the bar occupied, she hopped up on one in the middle, hooking her heels on the footrest.

The bartender braced his hands against the bar, hunching his shoulders. "What can I get you, sweetheart?"

"I'll take a club soda with some lime." She had no intention of sharing Samantha's fate.

His brows shot up. "If you're thirsty, why don't you go to the quick mart on the next block? You can get a sixty-four-ounce drink for a buck."

"Are you in business to sell drinks, or what?" She slapped a five-dollar bill on the bar.

He shrugged and filled a glass with club soda. He jabbed a slice of lime with a cocktail toothpick, dropped it into the clear, fizzing liquid and added a straw. "That's two-fifty."

She slid her money toward him and sipped her drink.

When he wandered past her again, she said, "Were you working when that woman was in here yesterday? The woman who died in the accident?"

He crossed his arms and leaned against the register behind him. "You a cop?"

Before coming to work for Tempest, that question would've been ludicrous since she favored heavy black eyeliner, black nail polish, tight jeans and boots most of the time. Her slacks, sensible heels and demure makeup made it a reasonable query.

"I'm not a cop. The woman was my friend." She dabbed her eyes with a cocktail napkin and didn't even have to fake it.

"Sorry." He stroked his beard. "The cops were around this morning trying to put blame on my bar for serving her excessive drinks. I told them and I'm telling you, she had two drinks in here last night and a whole lotta food. I had her credit card receipt to show them."

"I didn't think that sounded like her. Could someone else have been buying her drinks, maybe promising her a ride home that didn't pan out?"

"I have no clue. Her group sort of drifted away one-by-one, and she and another guy stayed later."

"Was he a regular here?"

"Not here. I figured he was part of the work group." He tapped her glass. "Can you handle another club soda or did you just come around for some answers?"

"I guess I just wanted to find out for myself what happened." She jabbed her straw into the ice at the bottom of the glass. "Did she leave with that guy?"

"I didn't notice, and my waitresses couldn't tell the cops, either. Just sad all the way around."

She slid from the stool and pocketed a buck-fifty, leaving a dollar bill on the bar. "Thanks."

"Hey."

She turned at the door.

"Drive carefully. I don't want this place getting a bad reputation."

"Thanks for your concern." She stepped into the cold air and shivered. If Samantha had two drinks only, her autopsy would show that level of alcohol in her system. Had the stranger slipped her something?

She refused to believe the coincidence of Samantha getting into a car accident on the very day Meyers returned that button to her. Tempest had long tentacles, and she could feel them tightening.

It was still early, and the happy hour crowd hadn't descended on the bar yet. The Tempest employees probably wouldn't be up for cocktails after Samantha's accident. Management hadn't called another all-hands meeting to announce Samantha's death, but the news had spread like wildfire, anyway. Tempest probably wanted to distance itself from the accident and not remind people that two employees had died in a matter of days.

She pulled away from the curb, checking her rearview mirror. A small car appeared from around the corner a block behind her. She couldn't lose the car even if she wanted to, since her place was a straight shot down the highway. Unless she wanted to veer off toward the lake, it looked as if she'd have company on the way home.

Her clammy hands gripped the steering wheel as she accelerated. She sped past the turnoff to the lake, and her heart jumped when the car that she thought had been following her took the off-ramp.

She blew out a breath and turned up the radio. Who was the paranoid one now?

With absolutely nobody following her, she pulled into the parking lot of her apartment complex.

A text message came through her cell and she pounced on it. After reading an alert from her bank, she tossed her phone into her purse.

Liam did say he'd try to text her, although she had no idea how he planned to accomplish that. Maybe he'd fail the psych test—for not being psycho enough—and Tempest would kick him out. What kind of outfit did he work for that would send him into the lion's den? These people could do anything to him, and then who'd save him?

She grabbed her purse and pushed the car door open with her foot. If it came to it, she'd do her damnedest to save Liam herself.

She collected a few bills and a slick circular from her mailbox and then jogged upstairs to her place. She shoved the key in the dead bolt and froze. She always locked the dead bolt.

She tried the door handle, which was locked. Would the police come out if she told them she'd locked her dead bolt and it was now unlocked?

She pulled the key free from the dead bolt and stuck it in the door handle, turning it slowly.

The door creaked as she eased it open, pushing it wider. She hung on to the doorknob and poked her head into the living room. Holding her breath, her gaze tracked around the room. Nothing looked out of place, but that didn't mean anything.

She left the door open and stepped into the room, clutching her keys between her knuckles like a weapon.

She'd taught Liam a few computer tricks, and he'd taught her a few tricks of self-defense.

She crept into the room, thankful for the first time she'd chosen a one-bedroom place. She toed off her shoes in case she had to make a mad dash for the exit, and then tiptoed toward the hallway. She peered into the empty bathroom first and then scooped in a breath and braved the bedroom, even checking the closet and under the bed.

She rushed back to her front door, slammed and locked it. She stood with her back against the door, breathing heavily, surveying her living room. Nothing was out of place, and yet…something didn't feel right.

The blood rushed to her head, and she launched off the door, making a beeline for a small area rug on the floor in front of the gas fireplace. She dropped to her knees and swept the rug aside. Using her fingernails, she worked her fingers into a crack between two loose floorboards. She pulled one up and reached into the floor, heaving a sigh as her fingers brushed the edges of Patterson's notebook. She gripped the cover and pulled it free, shaking the dirt from the pages.

She had to show this to Liam. Maybe he could make some sense of Patterson's notations. Hugging the book to her chest, she rose to her feet.

She tossed the notebook onto her kitchen counter and grabbed a plastic container of leftover pasta from the fridge. She popped the lid and shoved it into the microwave.

She didn't know how much more of this cloak-and-dagger stuff she could take. Couldn't Liam's agency order an autopsy for Patterson? With her as an eyewitness, that could be enough to shut down Tempest.

Chewing her lip, she watched the bowl of pasta spin around in the microwave. She knew Liam had loftier goals than just closing down operations for Tempest. He wanted to dig at the truth. He wanted to know Tempest's purpose and design for its agents.

When the pasta was done, she dumped it on a plate, poured herself a glass of red wine to make up for the tee-totaling at the bar and sat down with Patterson's notebook open on the table.

Why had he gone back to his office, and why had Ginger been so afraid he'd get his hands on Meyers's badge? She must've had some reason to suspect Patterson's loyalty to Tempest.

Patterson had been a big deal, had been one of the people directly reporting to Mr. Romo, a geo-political strategy guy who pinpointed the trouble spots for Tempest. If he hadn't been on board with Tempest's plans, he could've just resigned. It had to be more than that. Or maybe once you worked for Tempest, the only way to quit was in a coffin.

Patterson's chicken scratch blurred on the page, and it had nothing to do with the wine. She needed a new set of eyes reading this thing. She needed Liam.

She stowed the notebook back in its hiding place and washed the dishes. Then she put a small load of laundry into the washing machine and sat down at her laptop.

Before taking the gig at Tempest, she'd contracted to design a video game for her friend's company. Over the next few hours as she coded explosive traps and hidden viruses, she wished she could do the same to the Tempest facility.

Yawning, she put away her work and checked her phone once more for a message from Liam. If he didn't think he could get through to her, he shouldn't have even raised her hopes. Now that sick feeling in the pit of her stomach wouldn't go away. What had happened at the psych eval?

She put her wineglass in the sink and gathered her clothes from the dryer, folding them into her laundry basket. She hoisted the basket, balanced it on one hip and shuffled to her bedroom, where she dropped the basket on the floor near her dresser.

She collected four pair of underwear in one hand and pulled open the top drawer of her dresser. She caught her breath, and the underwear fell to the floor.

She was no neat freak, but she always shoved her panties to the right side of the underwear drawer and her bras to the left. Now they intermingled in a silky, frothy, rainbow kaleidoscope. A rash of goose bumps danced up her arms. It wasn't the fact that someone had run his hands through her underwear that creeped her out, or even the fact that someone had been in her apartment—it was what it meant.

Tempest was on to her.

Chapter Eight

Liam crouched at the side of the track and raked through the dirt with his fingers until they met the smooth edges of the phone he'd buried there earlier.

Prospero and his boss, Jack Coburn, weren't expecting any calls from him while he was undercover at Tempest. In fact, he'd get yanked off this assignment in a matter of seconds if Coburn discovered his risky behavior. Right now he didn't care.

He turned his back to the housing unit and cupped his hand around the phone as he dialed Katie's number. Nobody expected the recruits to be out and about after the psych sessions, after the hypnosis and their first dosing with the T-101. They'd called it a vitamin, but he knew better.

Prospero had given him an antidote to the T-101, and he'd undergone intense training in resisting hypnosis. He'd been fully conscious through the entire ordeal, including the injection of the T-101.

This was going down, and it was going down hard.

After five rings, Katie picked up the phone, her "hello" breathless and tentative.

"It's Liam. Are you okay?"

"I'm not okay. Someone was here."

He gripped the phone. "Don't say another word. Walk outside or go sit in your car. I'll wait."

She sucked in a breath, and then he heard movement and rustling over the phone.

"I'm back."

"Are you sitting in your car?"

"I'm out by the pool."

"Is it safe?"

"There's a group of people out here. Why am I outside? Do you think the person who broke into my place bugged it?"

"Could be."

She swore under her breath. "That's all I need."

He wiped a hand across his brow. "You know for sure someone broke into your place? Why would they want to tip you off?"

"They probably don't want to tip me off. Whoever broke in was careful. I had my suspicions when I discovered the dead bolt wasn't locked, so I checked out everything, and nothing was out of place."

"Are you just going off the dead bolt, then?"

"You didn't let me finish. I didn't notice anything out of place until I went to put my laundry away. Then I saw that someone had messed up my lingerie drawer."

"Your lingerie drawer?"

She sighed. "You know, underwear, bras."

"Since when did you start folding underwear in your drawer or folding anything anywhere?"

She clicked her tongue. "I have a system in that drawer, and it was messed up."

"Who knew?"

"Are you taking this seriously, Liam?"

"Deadly. That's why you're outside crashing someone's pool party." He saw a light from the recruit housing and sidled up next to the fencing. "Maybe they suspect you because you and Samantha hung out."

"Maybe Dustin ratted us out, and Ginger put two and

two together—she intercepted me at the track and Dustin discovered you hanging around the parking garage just when I was leaving. She also asked me a bunch of questions about programming in general and my work in particular on the way back to the offices."

"It could be anything or nothing. She could be taking precautions, and now you need to do the same. You have to quit, Katie."

"I'm not quitting. I'm too close to breaching their firewalls. Do you know the damage I can do to that facility once I have their computer systems at my fingertips?"

"You're not going to do any damage if you're dead." His harsh tone grated against his own ears, and the silence on the other end of the line engulfed him in guilt. "I'm sorry, Katie-O. I'm just telling it like it is."

"I know the risks, just like you." She cleared her throat. "What happened today in the psych evaluation? Why'd it take you so long to call me?"

"This is my job. I'm on assignment."

"Answer the question, McCabe. What happened out there today?"

"Dr. Harris tried to hypnotize me."

She gasped. "Tried? You obviously didn't succumb or *you'd* be dead."

"I can resist hypnosis. I told her the same story about how I got into trouble with my SEAL team that I'd told before. I even embellished the violence a little to make her salivate and to make it appear that I'd been holding back before."

"She didn't suspect anything?"

"If she had, she wouldn't have had the nurse or whoever that was inject me with their secret formula."

"Liam!" She choked. "They injected you with something? What did it do to you? Are you okay?"

"It did nothing. I have the antidote running through my system already. The T-101 won't have any effect on me."

"T-101?"

"That's what Tempest calls this serum."

"And th-that's what made Sebastian crazy?"

"He's not the first agent to kill himself, Katie. Another agent, Adam Belchick, was the first, and another agent probably would've taken himself out if he hadn't been killed first."

"We have to save the rest of them, Liam. We can't allow Tempest to ruin their lives."

"I'm working on it, Katie-O, but it's hard when I'm worrying about you at the same time."

"Where are you? How'd you sneak out?"

"I'm at the track. Everyone's conked out, but I gotta go. Are you going to quit your job?"

"No. When is your assignment over? What's your goal?"

"Find out how Tempest plans to use these juiced-up agents and destroy its capacity to do so."

"That's my goal, too, and I'm aiming for the head honcho."

"Mr. Romo?"

"Yep."

"Have you ever seen him?"

"A few times. Have you?"

"He's off-limits to us."

"He's off-limits to us, too. Maybe he doesn't exist."

"Oh, he exists. Do you think you saw an imposter? Someone's calling the shots, and it's not Ginger Spann." He kicked at the root of a bush growing beside the fence. "Have you noticed that helipad on top of building S?"

"No."

"I think that's the way Romo gets on and off the facility."

"We need to stop this, Liam."

He heard someone shout in the background, and his heart flip-flopped. "What's that?"

"The party's getting rowdy out here. Anything else?"

"Just be careful."

"You, too."

He ended the call and dropped to his knees. As he kicked dirt over the hole where he'd placed the phone, he swore to himself.

Why'd he ever let that woman go? If she gave him another chance, he'd keep her close forever...if they both came out of this alive.

KATIE WALKED INTO the office, her gaze focused straight in front of her, looking neither right nor left. She didn't want to catch anyone's eye and have to wonder if he'd been running his hands through her underwear the day before.

Had someone seen her go into the Deluxe? What had they hoped to find at her place? Did Ginger realize that Patterson's notebook was missing? Did she even know he had a notebook? She had to get that thing to Liam. He'd know how to decipher it.

She'd taken on this assignment by herself with the expectation that she'd find out why Sebastian killed himself and then exact revenge for it. How quickly she'd come to rely on Liam as soon as she'd discovered his presence here.

But Liam was that kind of guy. She'd always been strong and independent, so it took a real alpha male to get her to give up control and rely on someone else. She'd met her match in Liam, and then he went away.

She should've been strong enough to adjust to that, too, but his abandonment had opened up all those old wounds of a mother who'd left her on the steps of St. Anthony's Catholic Church in Imperial Beach at three days old.

She scooted her chair closer to her desk and logged in to her computer. She had some bug fixes to attend to, but she planned to devote a big chunk of her day to breaking through Tempest's firewall.

She got so deeply into her work, the telephone ringing on her desk startled her, jangling her nerves.

"KC Locke, program development."

"KC, this is Ginger Spann, and I have a proposition for you."

Katie swallowed and peeled her tongue from the roof of her mouth. "Oh?"

"I've been hearing good things about your work and figured you were an excellent fit for this particular project."

"What project?" She pressed a palm to her chest to steady her fluttering heart. Was this some kind of trick?

"I'll let Mr. Romo explain it to you."

Katie closed her eyes. "Mr. Romo? It must be important."

"It's very important, and I believe you're the person to take it on."

"What about Frank?" Someone had to bring her boss's name into this discussion.

Ginger's laugh tinkled over the line. "Frank is a capable manager, but he's not at your level of programming knowledge, is he?"

Katie swallowed. What did Ginger know about her level? Had she been looking into her background? The background she'd carefully cleansed?

"I...well, all my work comes through Frank."

"You surprise me, KC. I thought you'd jump at the chance to do more than the bug fixes Frank hands off to you."

She would jump at this opportunity if she hadn't just witnessed Ginger murdering a coworker.

"Of course I'm interested, but I want to keep my job. I don't want Frank thinking I'm going over his head."

"I'll worry about Frank. Meet me in front of the executive elevator in fifteen minutes."

Ginger ended the call, not waiting for a response.

Katie slumped in her chair, biting her bottom lip. What did this all mean? It could be the perfect opportunity to get close to Mr. Romo and get the keys to the castle. Or it could end in disaster.

She sat up in her chair and exited a few programs. When had she ever been one to steer clear of disaster if it held out the tiniest bit of hope that she'd get what she wanted in the end?

Ten minutes later she was standing in front of the executive elevator, clasping a notepad to her chest. This elevator stopped at the floor that housed the executives' offices and above, including the top floor occupied by Mr. Romo. You needed a special access card to operate the elevator, which Ginger most certainly must have.

A sharp click of heels against the tile floor announced the woman's arrival, right on time.

"I hope you haven't been waiting long, but your early arrival shows your eagerness. I had expected a little more enthusiasm from you on the phone."

Katie lifted her shoulders to her ears, still gripping the notebook. "I'm new here. I don't want to get on the wrong side of Frank."

"Frank doesn't have a wrong side." Ginger flashed her card at the card reader and stabbed the call button. "He's reliable but a bit of a slug."

Katie had no intention of throwing her boss under the bus. This could all be some kind of test of her loyalty. "He's a good manager."

"Ah, KC." The elevator doors opened and Ginger gestured her through with a flourish of her arm. "Playing it safe."

With her coworkers dropping around her, what choice did she have?

When the doors closed, Katie turned to Ginger. "This is a programming project, I assume?"

"Yes, a very exciting one I think you'll enjoy."

"Why me?"

Ginger clicked her tongue. "We do a very thorough background check here at Tempest."

If Katie expected more of an explanation, the thin line of Ginger's lips put that to rest.

The elevator skimmed past the executive floor and came to rest on the top level. The helicopter pad Liam had mentioned must be right above this level on the roof.

The doors whisked open and Ginger pressed the button to keep them ajar. "After you."

Katie stepped into the hallway, her heels sinking into the plush carpet.

Ginger breezed past her, one finger in the air. "This way."

Katie followed her to the end of the hallway, past several closed doors. The hushed atmosphere had her whispering. "Does anyone else have an office up here?"

"Mr. Romo occupies all the offices on this floor." Ginger winked. "He likes to spread out when he works."

They had reached the end of the hallway, and Ginger tapped on a thick wooden door. The handle clicked, and KC glanced up and spotted the camera. Mr. Romo had seen their approach. He wouldn't take any chances.

Ginger ushered her into the office first, where the thick carpet continued to silence their footsteps.

Katie took two hesitant steps into the room while a man rose from a sofa on the side of the room, lifting his computer from his lap and holding it with both hands. "Come in, come in."

Katie didn't necessarily expect Mr. Romo to be seven

feet tall with steam coming out of his ears, but the middle-aged compact man with the friendly smile and neat beard took her by surprise. He'd looked bigger from afar. Only his eyes, a light blue, marked his appearance as anything but ordinary.

Ginger closed the door with a click. "Mr. Romo, this is KC Locke. KC, Mr. Romo."

Mr. Romo placed the laptop on a sofa cushion next to him and dusted his hands together. "A pleasure to meet you, KC. Please, take a seat."

Since he didn't offer to shake hands, Katie took a chair across from the sofa, and Ginger sat in a chair next to hers.

Her gaze darted around the comfortably appointed room, more a lounge than an office, and then settled again on Mr. Romo, who'd resumed his seat.

"Water, coffee?"

"No, thank you."

He clasped his hands around one knee. "You're probably wondering what this is all about. We tend to be rather secretive here at Tempest."

"Ms. Spann mentioned something about a programming project, but I'm not sure why you tapped me for it."

"Really?" Mr. Romo tilted his head, looking somewhat like a bird with his close-cropped black hair resembling downy feathers. "Come, come, KC, let's be blunt. You're a hacker, aren't you?"

Katie widened her eyes to feign surprise. She hadn't scrubbed that part of her background at all. She'd figured an organization like Tempest would be attracted to rather than repelled by any hint of criminal activity in someone's past.

Her instincts had paid off.

"I—is that a problem?" She waved her hand. "All that's in my past. I can assure you all my programming is on the level today."

Except for when I'm trying to breach your firewalls.

Mr. Romo and Ginger exchanged a glance, heavy with a meaning that eluded her. Then he sat forward, resting his elbows on his knees. "That's not a problem at all, KC. In fact, we're hoping you can use some of those…skills to help us out."

She drummed a pen against her notepad. "I'm not sure I understand."

Ginger reached across and patted her shoulder. "Don't look so nervous. We're not going to ask you to hack into a bank."

Mr. Romo's unnervingly light eyes actually twinkled when he laughed along with Ginger, as if he hadn't ordered the murder of two of his employees in the space of one week.

"Nothing like that at all. It is a little—" he steepled his fingers "—unorthodox, but then you know Tempest is an unorthodox organization."

Licking her lips, Katie pinned her hands between her bouncing knees. "What's the project?"

"It involves spying on our employees." Mr. Romo delivered the line with a smile still hovering about his mouth, as if this were a big joke among the three of them.

She could play that game to get on the inside. If Romo offered her unfettered access to the computer system, she could wreak a severe amount of havoc in no time. Then she and Liam could get the hell out of here.

"Is that legal?"

Ginger snorted. "You can drop the act, KC. We've looked at your file, and you didn't seem all that concerned about the legality of your actions before. Why worry about it now? You have Mr. Romo's approval. That's all you need."

"Then count me in." Katie leaned back in her chair and

spread her arms out to her sides. "And if this is some kind of trap, you got me."

"No trap, young lady, but I appreciate your caution." Mr. Romo pulled the computer back into his lap and started tapping on the keyboard.

"This does come with some hazard pay, right?" KC jumped from her chair and paced to the window overlooking the facility. She could just make out the recruits in training. "I'm taking a risk if an employee finds out and brings some government agency down on our heads. I'll be taking the fall, not you."

Without looking up from the laptop, Mr. Romo snapped his fingers in Ginger's direction. "Ms. Spann will see to that."

Katie glanced at Ginger, who stretched her lips into a smile. "Of course, KC. You'll be compensated for your efforts, but we expect to see results."

"Oh, I'll get you results. When do we start?"

"Right now." Mr. Romo tapped his laptop screen. "I want you to start with these two."

Katie sauntered across the room to the couch and leaned over Mr. Romo's shoulder.

The blood roared in her ears, and she stifled a gasp as she stared into the clear blue eyes of Liam McCabe.

Chapter Nine

Mr. Romo cranked his head around, his dark brows colliding over his nose. "What's wrong?"

Katie could feel Ginger practically breathing down her neck. She cleared her throat. "I've seen those two before."

"Where? They're recruits." Mr. Romo's pale gaze skewered her.

Ginger sat on the arm of the couch. "Did you see them at the all-hands meeting?"

"No." Liam wouldn't mind if she squealed on him to gain some street cred with these two. She took a deep breath. "I saw them out by the employee parking garage when I left the other night."

"What were they doing?" Mr. Romo's quiet tone sent a chill down her spine.

"They were just standing there talking. The one guy, the black guy, was smoking a cigarette." She jabbed her finger at Dustin's picture on the screen.

Had Liam misjudged Dustin? The recruit couldn't be spying for Romo if Romo wanted her to spy on Dustin. Or maybe she'd walked into one big trap.

"Did they say anything to you?" Ginger moved to her side and placed a hand on Katie's arm.

"We exchanged a few words. I guess the guy with the cigarette didn't want anyone to see him smoking."

"And the other one? The blond?" Mr. Romo flicked his manicured fingers at Liam's picture. "What excuse did he give?"

"I don't know. He didn't say much. Did they do something wrong? Why do you want me to spy on them?"

"You don't need to worry about that part, KC. We'll give the directions, and you'll follow. Do you think you can do that?" Ginger's fingers curled into her arm, her nails poking at the flesh beneath the material of her blouse.

Katie nodded. "Of course. How do you want me to monitor them?"

"Through their computer log-ins at first. Each recruit has a laptop and an access card. We want you to track what they're doing on their laptops—the obvious things like emails and websites visited and then anything else you can dig up, anything they might be trying to conceal."

"I can do that."

Ginger loosened her grip, and her touch turned into a caress. "We knew you could, KC, and we figured with your criminal background you wouldn't blink an eye at the request…if we held out a little monetary incentive."

Standing up, she broke away from Ginger. "Criminal background?"

"Well, you did lie to us about your past activities, about your juvenile crimes, didn't you?" Ginger shook her finger in her face. "That in itself is a crime—fraud."

"Are you threatening me?" Katie widened her stance and crossed her arms across her chest and wildly beating heart. Ginger played hardball.

Mr. Romo stood up between them, hands out. "Let's dispense with the ugliness and be frank. If you don't tell on us, we won't tell on you. That gives us all a little skin in this game, but a whole lot to gain."

He cupped his hands and gestured to them to move in closer. Ginger took a step toward him, and he curled his arm around her waist and pulled her next to him. "Your turn, KC."

Katie suppressed a shiver and shuffled toward him. Putting his arm around her waist, he dragged her into the circle. Ginger sidled up next to her and wrapped her arm around Katie's waist, as well.

As much as she wanted to, Katie couldn't stand there with her arms hanging at her sides so she put one around Mr. Romo, holding on to his suit jacket with two fingers and placing the other lightly around Ginger's back.

Mr. Romo tightened the circle by pulling them so close, Katie could make out white flecks in the irises of his blue eyes. Was that what made them so light?

"Ginger and I are in this together to do what needs to be done to protect Tempest, and as a result make this world a better place, and we're happy to have you along for the ride, KC." His hand slipped from her waist to her hip, his fingers resting on the curve of her backside.

Her stomach roiled, and she had a sudden urge to puke in the middle of the circle of trust. And she would have except for the stronger urge to warn Liam that Mr. Romo had him in his crosshairs.

LIAM SAT IN the back of the classroom and logged in to his laptop. Physical training this morning had been exhausting. He'd had to keep up with all the recruits who'd had their first dose of T-101 the day before.

He'd have to wrap up his work here soon or it would become apparent that the T-101 was not having its desired effect on him.

As soon as his computer powered up, he launched the instant messenger. He didn't expect to see any messages from Katie. She'd warned him that her messages might pop up automatically when he logged in and he might not be alone when they did.

He looked around the room at the other recruits logging in to complete assignments left over from yesterday because of their extralong psych evaluations. As far as he knew from questioning the other recruits, he'd been the only one subjected to hypnosis. The psychologists might be using different methods for different recruits, or he'd been singled out.

He typed a message to Katie.

You there?

Apparently, she'd been singled out, too, if they'd searched her apartment. As he stared at the blinking cursor, he wondered what her place looked like.

Back in San Diego, she'd had a mishmash of stuff in her apartment. She'd called her tastes eclectic, but he'd come to the conclusion she had no specific taste at all. She just loved stuffing her apartment with all the odds and ends she'd collected on her travels—items to remind her of the places she'd been.

She'd make a boatload of money as an independent contractor hiring out her programming skills, and then take off for a month or two—until she'd met him. Then she'd been ready to settle down and like an idiot, he'd taken off. Sure, his team had needed him, but it never occurred to him that Katie-O had needed him more.

She'd been the epitome of the cool chick—casual, rootless, free-spirited. She'd sported a stud on the side of her nose then, a pierced belly button and that mermaid tattoo. How the hell was he supposed to know that he'd break her heart by leaving?

But he did know, deep down. Katie put on that tough-girl act because that's what she'd needed to do in the past to get by. She'd let her guard down enough with him so that he could see the soft squishy insides beneath the hard shell.

And he'd let her down. He'd be damned if he'd do it again.

The screen flickered and a message popped up.

They're on to you.

He jerked his head up and scanned the room. He asked her how she knew that, and his heart pounded while he waited for her response.

Five minutes later she replied.

We need to meet tonight.

Stairwell?

Parking structure at 9.

The rest of the afternoon and early evening passed in a blur of assignments, tests and nutritional guidance, which was a joke. Who needed good nutrition when you were being jacked up with some chemical formula that altered the composition of your brain and body?

During their downtime after dinner, most of the guys watched TV or played video games—probably a few of Katie's designs. The pool and Jacuzzi stayed open all night, and some of the guys wandered around the facility for a change of scenery. He'd be wandering around the facility, too, the parking structure to be exact.

At ten minutes to nine, he slipped out of the recruits' compound and hugged the edges of the buildings on his way to the employee parking structure. He'd better not see Dustin Gantt out for a smoke again.

He headed for the same spot where he'd seen Katie yesterday and ducked into the shadows.

A few minutes later she appeared at the edge of the

quad and strode toward the parking structure. When she got within a few feet of him, he whispered her name.

She didn't even break her stride. "Follow me upstairs to my car."

"Cameras?"

"Not a problem."

They didn't say another word as they marched up the stairs to the second level of the structure. A lone car huddled in a space in the middle of the lot, and as Katie aimed her remote at it, the lights blinked once in welcome.

He climbed into the passenger seat of the small car and shoved the seat back as far as it would go, and he still had to bend his knees. "Could you find a smaller car?"

"I paid cash for it and never registered it—just another way to cover my tracks."

"You'd make a better Tempest agent than half those recruits." He jerked his thumb over his shoulder.

"Not once they get all juiced up." She grabbed his arm. "I have all kinds of news for you."

"I figured you did. How do you know they're on to me?"

"I'm working with them."

His eyebrows shot up. "What does that mean?"

"I met Mr. Romo, Liam. I'm in. He and Ginger want me to join the dark side and start spying on Tempest employees. I'm thinking that's why they broke into my apartment and maybe even bugged it, but it looks like I passed with flying colors."

"I don't know, Katie-O. That doesn't sound safe. They could be playing you."

Her nails dug deeper into his flesh. "You're the one who's not safe, Liam. They want me to spy on you."

His eyelid twitched. He'd failed. His first assignment for Prospero and he'd failed. "Why? Did they indicate what had made them suspicious?"

She flicked the keys in the ignition. "They're not going

to let me in on those details. I did tell them I'd seen you and Dustin by the parking structure the other night."

"Great. Thanks."

"I wanted to ingratiate myself with them, let them know they hadn't made a mistake by approaching me. They already suspected you, anyway."

"And Dustin."

"Yeah, looks like you were wrong about him."

"Maybe, maybe not." He covered her hand resting on the steering wheel with his. "Like I said, maybe they're playing you. Maybe they're playing both of us, and Dustin is in on the gig."

"I don't think so, Liam. They're giving me the keys to the castle."

"Computer access?" He squeezed her hand.

"They want me to start with you and Dustin. It's perfect."

"If it's not a setup." He traced the ridges of her knuckles. "What's he like, Romo?"

"Ordinary except for his eyes. They're such a light blue, especially for his coloring. He has black hair and an olive skin tone."

"Maybe they're contacts just to freak people out."

"I don't think he needs the eyes for that." She huffed out a breath. "I'm going to use my newfound freedom to poke at their firewalls. I'm going to find out their master plan."

"Did they wonder why you jumped in with both feet and no questions asked?"

"I made it about money and they made it about blackmail."

"Blackmail?"

"I lied about my background on my application and during the interview. Ginger implied they could file charges or something."

"I don't think so."

"I pretended to believe her, anyway. They couldn't exactly threaten my life if I didn't play along, although you and I both know that's the takeaway."

Knots tightened in his belly. "You're in over your head, Katie-O. Just leave. Now."

Her jaw dropped. "No way. I have them right where I want them."

"You know what these people are capable of. They can make you believe whatever they want you to believe."

Turning toward him, she placed her hands on his thigh. "This gives me a chance to protect you, too. If they suspect you, I can throw them off your scent."

"You don't need to protect me, Katie." He threaded his fingers through hers. "Protection is my job, and I know I blew it before, but I'm not going to make that mistake again."

Her lashes fluttered against her smooth cheeks. "I wasn't in any danger when you left me to do another tour."

"You were in danger of erecting your hard shell again. I'd broken through. I'd made you feel safe and loved, and then I snatched all that away." He skimmed the pad of his thumb along her jaw. "And I never even said I was sorry."

"You did what you had to do." She shrugged, and he put his hands on her raised shoulders.

"Don't. Don't pretend it didn't hurt. Don't pretend I didn't betray your trust, your…love."

Her chest rose and fell as she twisted her fingers in her lap. "Liam, I…"

He held his breath, waiting for the words he'd needed to hear from her two years ago.

Instead, an explosion rocked the car and lit up the night sky.

Chapter Ten

The blast slammed Katie's head against the seat and seemed to lift the car.

"Liam!"

His arms came around her. "My God. Are you okay?"

"What was that? What happened?"

"It was some kind of explosion, and it was close." He pointed to the gaps between the parking structure levels. "I can see the smoke."

She covered her ears, which were pounding. "We have to get out of here. We can't be seen together."

He pulled her into his arms and kissed her hard on the mouth. "Be careful. I'm not losing you again."

Then he slipped out of the car and disappeared.

She sat, gripping the steering wheel for a few minutes, frozen. She couldn't just drive out of the structure as if nothing had happened. She had every right to be here, since she'd worked late.

She got out of the car on shaky legs, and the acrid smell of smoke engulfed her. She choked and headed for the stairwell.

Sirens wailed in the distance. Someone had already called the fire department.

She headed toward the side of the parking structure and peeked through the gaps. Gasping, she jumped back.

Flames engulfed one side of the small building across the way, and chunks of cement and twisted metal littered the quad.

It had to have been a bomb. Had Tempest figured out a new way to get rid of more pesky employees?

The blare of the sirens drew closer, and Katie hit the stairwell and jogged down the steps. At least Liam had been with her at the time of the explosion, so she didn't have to worry about him.

His words had turned her insides to jelly and made her breathless until the blast had ruined the moment. It had brought them both back to reality. They needed each other right now—not as lovers but as colleagues.

When she reached the bottom of the structure, she pressed her palms against the metal door. When she'd peered from above, she hadn't noticed the fire threatening the parking garage, and the door still felt cool to the touch.

She cracked it open. The debris and smoke in the air made her eyes water, and she squinted at the mayhem the blast had caused. The fire trucks had reached the scene, and knots of people clustered on the outskirts of the quad.

Covering her mouth and nose with one hand, she pushed through the door and picked her way across smoldering chunks of the building and shards of glass.

"Ma'am! Ma'am! Are you all right?"

One of the firemen had spotted her and rushed to her side. "You need to keep your distance."

"I'm fine. I was in the parking structure, in my car." She stumbled, and the fireman caught her arm.

"KC? Oh, my God, are you okay?" Ginger flew toward her, grabbing her hand. "Is there anyone else in the garage?"

Apparently, she'd become Ginger's new best friend once she'd decided to spy for her and Mr. Romo, and her new bestie seemed genuinely shocked by the scene around them. If the Tempest cabal hadn't engineered this little bonfire, who had?

Liam's agency wouldn't be this in-your-face. He'd already explained that they were forming a trap around Tempest and would wait it out for the proof.

"KC?" Ginger squeezed her hand. "Anyone else?"

Katie shook some soot and white powder from her hair. "N-no. I didn't see any other people or cars in the parking structure. I was already in my car, but I had to see what was going on. Does anyone know what happened?"

"One of the firemen mentioned something about a gas line here. I hope nobody else was burning the midnight oil, like you."

"I didn't see anyone. What blew up?" She eyed the main office building, which had a few broken windows but no other damage.

"It was the small utility building next to the parking structure."

"Were all these people in the main building?" She nodded toward the clutches of people, murmuring together and staring at the scene with shocked faces.

"A few of them. Everyone got out safely, as far as we know. No injuries, nobody in the utility building. The guys over there are the recruits. I think they felt the explosion all the way across the facility. They certainly heard it."

Katie scanned the crowd of men near the fire engines and let out a breath when she saw Liam's face among them. Of course, he'd be here just like all the rest of them.

She touched Ginger's arm. "Mr. Romo? Is he okay?"

"He's fine. The building rocked a bit but he's high enough that the explosion didn't affect him or any of the windows in his office. He got out quickly, though. We both did." Ginger covered her hand with her long, tapered fingers. "He made quite an impression on you, didn't he?"

Katie tipped her chin to her chest. "He's the type of man who commands a room."

"He certainly does. Women want him and men want to be him, as the saying goes." She stroked Katie's fingers and held her gaze, her glossed lips parted.

Katie looked away as heat surged up her chest and burned her cheeks. Was Ginger coming on to her or suggesting that *she* wanted Mr. Romo? She hadn't known what to make of that weird group hug in Mr. Romo's office, but his wandering hands had grossed her out.

Ginger gave a low chuckle and pinched Katie's chin. "Don't worry about it, KC. Mr. Romo has that effect on all women. But rest assured, he's safe and secure right now and will be happy to hear you're the same."

Katie swallowed. "I'm sure he'll be relieved that *all* of his employees got out safely."

"Of course, but especially you, KC." Ginger had turned to watch the firemen douse the flames with their hoses, her sharp profile in relief against the orange glow of the fire. "You're one of us, now."

Ginger strode toward the other employees, waving her arms and barking orders. Katie slumped. What the hell had she gotten herself into?

Liam returned to his housing unit along with the other recruits still yammering about the explosion. If they all really believed some faulty gas line caused that blast, they didn't deserve to be covert ops agents. Given the current climate here, if Tempest hadn't set off that explosion, one of its enemies did.

He'd meant what he said to Katie, that she'd make a better agent than half these guys. It didn't surprise him that Ginger Spann had recognized how valuable Katie's skills could be to an organization like Tempest. It didn't surprise him, but it did worry the hell out of him. She'd officially entered the lion's den, and he'd do everything within his power to make sure she came out of it without a bite.

"Hey, man, you up for some Worldwide War?" Charlie jerked his thumb at the video game room.

"I'm dead tired but knock yourself out." He slipped into his room and flicked on the light. His gaze swept across the four corners of the ceiling. Katie had assured him that she could take care of any cameras or bugs, especially now that she'd been invited into the inner circle.

He still planned to watch his back. Ginger Spann and Mr. Romo had obviously made him, or at least they had their suspicions. What had tipped them off?

Dr. Harris—it must've had something to do with his session with her yesterday. Maybe he'd gone overboard in proclaiming his love of violence and rebellion.

He stripped down to his boxers, tossing the notebook Katie had pressed into his hands while they were in her car onto the bed, and ducked into the bathroom to brush his teeth and splash some water on his face. He could use a shower to get rid of the acrid stench of the fire that lingered in his skin and hair, but beneath that smell lurked another scent—wildflowers and warm California sunshine.

Katie-O's lips had felt soft and juicy beneath his. The kiss had been natural and right—and he planned to repeat it.

He shut off the lights overhead and clicked on the lamp clipped to the headboard of his bed. He crawled between the sheets, his head sinking against the pillow. He closed his eyes for a few seconds and then dragged Garrett Patterson's notebook into his lap.

Katie had confessed she couldn't make heads or tails out of Patterson's notes, but Patterson must've wanted to protect the information or he wouldn't have hidden it beneath his desk blotter.

Ginger and Romo probably didn't have a clue that this notebook even existed. Patterson must've been hiding it from his bosses.

He flipped open the cover. For all he knew it could be a detailed accounting of all the women Patterson had sexually harassed at Tempest.

His gaze ran down the first page—numbers and more numbers. Prospero had required training in code-breaking...and he'd been at the top of the class. Katie should excel at this sort of thing, but she'd always maintained she didn't have the patience to review or fix anyone else's software codes. Her mind always leaped ahead to how she'd create it from scratch.

He trailed his index finger along the columns of numbers in decimals. Another column next to that one contained sets of four numbers.

He rubbed his eyes and brought the notebook closer to his face. Snorting, he smacked the paper. He wouldn't even call this set of numbers a code. The four numbers clearly represented dates—months and days, no years. Katie must be slipping.

He studied the dates, which meant nothing to him—no holidays, nothing of significance. He'd have to run them on his laptop, which Katie had also promised to protect.

He stared at the other numbers through half-closed eyelids and then gave up. His brain was as blurry as his eyesight at this point.

He dragged himself out of bed and slid a dime from his nightstand. He climbed on top of the bed, reaching for the vent in the ceiling. Using the dime, he unscrewed the plate over the vent and then shoved the notebook in the open space. He replaced the vent and dropped back onto the bed.

He'd have to get Prospero something they could use and

quick. He couldn't fake one more dose of T-101. Tempest would either expel him for not being susceptible to the formula…or they'd kill him.

THE FOLLOWING MORNING his alarm startled him awake. He rolled onto his back and eyed the vent—GPS coordinates. The first set of numbers indicated locations and the second set, dates. Why would Patterson be hiding that information from Mr. Romo?

He rolled out of bed, took a quick shower and dressed in gym clothes. They had a five-mile run this morning before breakfast. After that it was anyone's guess what they'd do. If Tempest had planned and executed that little fireworks display last night, there would be some fallout from it—maybe another conveniently dead body.

At least it wouldn't be Katie's.

He joined a couple of the other recruits in the hallway and they headed out to the track together.

Liam started stretching and warming up in the chilly morning air. Hamilton liked them all to start together, so the guys scattered on the grass waited for the slow starters to show up.

Liam rose from his stretch and sprinted up the bleachers. At the top he peered across the facility to the damaged building. Would the employees be going to work in their building with the broken windows today? The fire department probably gave them the all-clear already. The windows were boarded and the debris shoved off to the side.

He glanced at the field where Mills and Hamilton had their heads together, and a ripple of excitement ran through the recruits.

Now what?

He jogged down the bleachers and approached Charlie talking with two other guys.

"What's going on? How come we haven't started the run yet?"

Charlie raised an eyebrow. "Dustin Gantt is missing, dude, and they think he blew up the building last night to escape."

Chapter Eleven

"So you were right about him. I'm only sorry you didn't approach me sooner. Maybe I could've prevented this." Katie sat in a chair across the room from Mr. Romo and Ginger, with her knees together, hands folded in her lap.

Ginger paced the room, sparks of rage shooting from her green eyes. "You saw him in that area the other night, didn't you, him and McCabe? They must've been setting it all up then."

"McCabe?" Katie drew her brows over her nose. "Is he missing, too?"

"Exactly, Ginger." Mr. Romo clicked his tongue. "If the two of them were involved in this together, McCabe would've escaped with Gantt."

"I don't like it. I don't like him." She wedged her hand on one slim hip. "We thought he'd be a perfect specimen. He far outpaced the other recruits in every physical pursuit. So why didn't the T-101 have the desired effect?"

Katie blinked. She wasn't supposed to know what T-101 was. "T-101?"

Mr. Romo shot Ginger a look that could freeze her on the spot if she weren't already as cold as ice. "A highly concentrated vitamin supplement we administer to the recruits to improve their physical prowess."

"Oh." Katie spread her hands. "Maybe it didn't do anything for him because he's already at the top of his game."

"Are you an expert on health and nutrition now, KC?" Ginger strolled toward Mr. Romo and dropped a hand on his shoulder in a proprietary way.

Did Ginger think she had designs on the irresistible Mr. Romo? She seemed to encourage it on the one hand, and now she'd gone all territorial on her...and him.

Katie was still trying to process Dustin's betrayal of Tempest. What did it mean? Maybe Liam's agency wasn't the only one trying to infiltrate Tempest. But if Dustin was working for someone else, what good did that blast do other than afford him a distraction to escape?

Dustin must've figured out enough about Tempest to realize that a recruit couldn't just up and quit at this point in the training.

Ginger snapped her fingers. "Are you listening?"

"Sorry, I was thinking about the best way to track Gantt's computer use."

Mr. Romo almost beamed at her. "You see, Ginger, our girl is on it."

Katie flashed him a broad smile, but her stomach did a flip. "I do have a question, if you don't mind. Why didn't Dustin Gantt just quit? Why go through all that trouble to leave Tempest?"

Mr. Romo shifted his light gaze toward Ginger. "It's in their contract. Once they reach a certain point in their training, they lose a large portion of their signing bonus."

She shrugged. "Just seems kind of extreme to me."

Mr. Romo tapped his head. "Dustin Gantt had issues, obviously."

"Do you even know for sure he's the one who did it? Maybe it's just a coincidence—the explosion and his departure."

"KC, we're not paying you to theorize. We're paying

you to spy." She clapped her hands twice. "Now, go find out what Gantt was up to before he made his spectacular exit. We expect a report back at the end of the day."

"I'm on it." Damn, she'd appeared too eager, but any normal person would have questions.

Mr. Romo beckoned her with a cupped hand. "Come here, KC."

Katie forced her legs to move, although they felt like lead. She approached Mr. Romo's realm, just close enough to encounter a wave of his spicy cologne. Then she planted her feet in the dense carpet.

His lip twitched but his blue eyes looked like chips of ice. Then he rose slowly from the couch and gathered her in his arms, again resting one hand against the curve of her hip.

Every muscle in Katie's body tensed as her arms hung at her sides.

Mr. Romo gave her a squeeze and then released her. She stumbled back.

"I'm a hugger." He lifted one powerful shoulder. "Isn't that right, Ginger?"

Ginger laughed. "I think you're a little overwhelming for *our girl*, Mr. Romo."

Katie gritted her teeth. In normal circumstances, she'd haul off and smack Mr. Romo in the face. But these weren't normal circumstances, and these weren't normal people. Did Ginger call him Mr. Romo while she was straddling him in bed, too?

"I—I'm just not used to hugging in a work environment."

Ginger took two long steps toward her and cupped her face with one hand. "You're not used to much hugging or personal contact at all, are you? You poor, lost lamb. We know all about your background in the foster care system, shunted from one uncaring home to another. We're going to make that all go away for you, KC. You have a place with us."

As long as you do what we tell you to do.

The unspoken thought hung in the air between them, but Katie heard it as clearly as if Ginger had shouted it in her ear.

"I appreciate that, Ginger."

Ginger's touch on her cheek turned into a caress. "We'll take care of you, KC. Now get to work, dear."

Katie backed out of Mr. Romo's office and then sped down the hallway to the executive elevator. Ginger had paused it, so all Katie had to do was punch the button for her floor.

When the doors closed, she slumped against the wall of the elevator car, a bead of sweat trickling down the back of her neck.

What kind of game were these two playing?

She had no doubt Ginger and Mr. Romo had a thing going on, but what role did they expect her to play in their relationship?

Ginger alternately acted jealous and seductive.

When the elevator landed on her floor, she squared her shoulders and strode to her cubicle. As if she didn't have enough incentives to wrap up this job, the prospect of working with Romo and Ginger on a daily basis just amped up her motivation tenfold.

Liam must know about Dustin, but what did he think about his defection? The man had been playing a part when she'd run into him and Liam near the parking structure. He must've been worried that she and Liam would report him. Was that why he acted when he did? He'd destroyed the maintenance building but hadn't done much more damage than that. Had he been planning an attack on a larger scale but abandoned it because Liam had discovered him?

She'd do her research on Dustin, all right, but she had

no intention of turning any findings over to Mr. Romo. If Dustin Gantt had any info about Tempest's nefarious plans, Liam would want to know about it.

She pulled her chair up to her computer and glanced at the time in the lower right-hand corner of her screen. The recruits should be in the classroom about now, but she never texted Liam first in case someone was hovering over his laptop.

He'd wasted no time, though. When she launched her instant messenger, a note was waiting from Liam. One word:

Dustin?

She explained to him that the official word was that he was off the rails and caused a disruption to escape the facility and break his contract.

He responded:

Same here. Need to see you.

She assured him that she could arrange that. After all, wasn't she part of the inner circle now?

A few hours later, after clearance from Ginger, Katie made her way to the training facility. She had some work to do on the recruits' laptops.

Ginger had already called ahead for her, so when she entered the classroom, Mills didn't blink an eye. He glanced up from his desk once and said, "Do what you have to do. Gantt's computer is the one in the third row."

She retrieved the laptop. "I'm going to take this into the empty classroom next door, and I'm going to have to get a couple of these guys to leave class and join me with their laptops."

"No problem. They're doing independent study right now. Just call 'em out as you need 'em."

"Thanks." She tucked Dustin's laptop under her arm and left the classroom without stealing one look at Liam.

After giving Gantt's laptop the once-over, she'd call another recruit in here first to keep suspicion away from Liam.

She checked the obvious on Dustin's computer—browsing history, cookies, files. The guy was no idiot, but everyone left a trail on their computers whether they knew it or not, and not every hacker knew how to reveal that hidden history—but she did.

She'd have to do the heavy work back at her office. She powered off his laptop and snapped the lid shut.

Then she checked her list and decided to call in Charlie Beck for the hell of it. She poked her head into the classroom where the recruits were clicking away on their keyboards. "Charlie Beck?"

A young guy looked up from his work, eyes wide, cheeks flushed.

Wow, did she strike the same fear into the hearts of Tempest employees as Ginger Spann did? She'd truly reached inner-circle status. Mr. Romo would be so proud, he'd likely give her another hug. So she'd better keep this to herself.

"Sh-should I bring my laptop?" Charlie stood, halfway crouched over his desk.

"That's the point, cowboy."

Charlie's blush deepened at the scattered guffaws from his fellow recruits.

He followed her into the other classroom, carrying his laptop awkwardly in front of him.

She patted the desk next to hers. "Just put it here."

"Are we all under some kind of investigation because of Dustin Gantt?"

"Not really, nothing to worry about, but honestly, if you

think you might want to break your contract it's best just to talk it out instead of blowing things up and running away."

"Oh, yeah, hell, I'd never do that."

She pointed to his laptop. "Could you please log in to your computer?"

"Uh, I didn't log out. I just closed it."

She suppressed a sigh and smiled. She didn't want to be another Ginger. "That's perfect. Just wake it up and we'll get to work."

Charlie had been working on a paper about political unrest in several West African countries.

She waved her hand at the document. "You can close out of this and open your browser."

He saved the file and launched a browser. "Do you need me to do anything else?"

"Just switch places with me."

"Sure." He clambered out of the chair that was too small for his long, lanky frame and held out the chair for her.

"Thanks." She settled herself in front of Charlie's laptop and opened his browsing history just to look busy. A number of porn sites cropped up in the list.

He coughed. "You know, some of the other guys were messing around with my laptop. I didn't visit those websites."

"I don't care." She flicked her fingers at the screen. "That's not what I'm here for, anyway. I'm just making sure you don't have a particular virus on your computer, but those are just the types of websites that harbor bugs and viruses."

"I didn't know that. I'll make sure those guys don't get to my computer again."

"Also, you can never really delete your browsing history, so you'd better be careful." She cleared her throat. "I mean, those other guys need to be careful."

"Yeah, yeah. I'll put out the word."

She could've eased Charlie's fears since she didn't think Mr. Romo would care if the recruits were visiting porn sites, just as long as they all took their vitamins and turned into good little robots.

She checked out a few more areas of Charlie's computer, actually found some malware, probably from those porn sites, and ran a fix.

"I think that'll do it." She restarted his computer. "So, what's everyone saying about Dustin Gantt?"

"We can't believe it. I can't believe it. He seemed like a cool guy, really gung-ho. He was the only one who came close to McCabe in the physical fitness department, until that last day."

"His last day of PT?" She unplugged Charlie's laptop and snapped the lid closed for him.

"Yeah, he really lagged behind. McCabe, too. They both seemed slower that day. Hell, even I did more pull-ups than McCabe. That was a first for me."

"Maybe Gantt just lost interest and decided to split and make a splash while he did so."

Maybe the T-101 didn't have an effect on Dustin, but he must've been planning his escape before the injection of the drug.

"I don't know. Crazy way to go out." He scooped his laptop from the desk. "You finished?"

"You're good to go. Can you please send Liam McCabe in here with his laptop?"

"Sure." He turned at the door. "Ms. Locke? You're not going to mention those websites, are you?"

She ran her fingertip across the seam of her lips. "My lips are sealed."

"Thanks, ma'am."

She paced the room for the next several minutes until Liam came through the door. It took an iron will not to rush across the room and throw herself at him. He looked so damned good and safe and normal. She needed a huge dose of normal right now after slinking out of Mr. Romo's lair.

Liam snapped the door closed behind him. "How'd you manage this visit?"

"In addition to collecting Dustin's laptop, I told them I could put some tracking software on yours."

He walked to the desk where she had her purse and set his computer on top of it. "My stomach's been in knots thinking about you with those two. I just can't get past the idea that they're on to you and setting you up for something."

"I really don't think so, Liam." She had no intention of telling him about the creepy sexual vibe she'd been getting from both Ginger and Mr. Romo. He didn't need anything else to worry about.

He pointed to his laptop. "Shouldn't we at least pretend to be working on the computer in case someone comes in here?"

"Yeah, although I requested privacy." She took a seat at the desk, and he pulled up a chair next to hers.

She turned the laptop toward him. "Go ahead and log in."

He reached past her, and she watched his strong fingers move across the keyboard while she inhaled his fresh scent. He didn't need any heavy cologne to increase his allure.

He glanced her way. "Anything else?"

She blinked and focused on the screen. "Nope." She accessed his browsing history, hoping not to find any porn sites there. "You were wrong about Dustin. What do you think about him now?"

"I'm not sure. Maybe something happened here that spooked him. The T-101 injection could've been the last straw, and maybe he's not susceptible to hypnosis so he was able to put two and two together."

"The T-101 didn't have any effect on his system."

"How do you know that? I didn't notice."

"Charlie told me. You were probably too concerned about your own behavior to notice Dustin's." She skimmed the websites he'd visited. "No porn."

"Excuse me?" His brows shot up, disappearing beneath the lock of sandy-blond hair that fell over his forehead.

"That idiot Charlie had been visiting porn sites on his company laptop. Who does that?"

"An idiot." He ran a hand through his hair. "So, Dustin got freaked out by a few things, figured Tempest wouldn't let him out of his contract and caused a distraction to escape. I plan to look him up when we get out of here, but I have something else to tell you."

She jerked her head to the side. "What?"

"I figured out the code in Patterson's notebook, which really wasn't much of a code."

"You did?" Leaning over, she took his face in her hands. "I knew I could count on you. I looked at it for two minutes and got dizzy."

He turned his head, placing his lips against her palm. "Patience is not your strong suit, Katie-O."

"Ain't that the truth? What did all those numbers mean?" The kiss had scorched her flesh, and she dropped her hands into her lap, curling that hand into a fist as if to capture the kiss for later inspection.

"They're GPS coordinates and dates—months and days."

She slumped in her chair. "I missed that? Seems kind of obvious now. Where are the locations, and what's the significance of the dates?"

"That's—" he reached over to the keyboard and launched a search engine "—what I'm hoping we can discover right now. Anything we put in here, you can get rid of, right? Nobody will know I've been looking up those coordinates on my computer?"

"Just call me the cleaner." She huffed on her fingernails and polished them on the front of her blouse.

"You know what I'm going to miss most about being here at Tempest with you?" He flicked her collar. "These blouses and slacks."

She smacked his hand away. "This is proper office attire."

He grinned the grin that had reeled her in from the moment she'd met him at Sebastian's party over three years ago.

"You ready for those coordinates now?"

"Do you have the notebook?"

He tapped his head. "It's all in here. Ready?"

"Show-off." She positioned her fingers on the keyboard. "Shoot."

He reeled off the first set, and she entered the coordinates into the website she'd accessed.

Hunching forward, Liam peered at the monitor. "Djibouti, the capital city of the Republic. Follow up on that address."

She entered the address for the African city and read aloud. "That's the address of the Parliament Building there."

He poked at the screen. "Get another tab going and input this date."

She clicked open a new browser page and typed in the date that Liam recited from the recesses of his photographic memory. She scanned the bits and pieces on the screen. "Nothing."

"Okay, enter that date along with the Parliament Building in Djibouti."

This time the search engine returned several news stories about two African leaders who'd been killed when their cars had exploded as they were leaving a meeting at the Parliament Building in Djibouti.

She covered her mouth and turned to Liam. "Do you think Tempest was responsible for that?"

"Let's do the next one."

He gave her a location, and this time it came back to Montevideo in Uruguay. When they matched the location, a street in a gated community, to the date, they got no hits.

Liam wouldn't give up. He continued to rattle off different search combinations until a news story about the death of a prominent Uruguayan judge popped up.

She let out a breath. "Tempest's handiwork again. What are they trying to accomplish with these assassinations besides the obvious?"

"I don't know, but the two dates we entered occurred in the past. Patterson's dates included month and day only, no year, so I just assumed the dates took place this year. There are dates on those notebook pages still in the future."

She clasped the back of her neck and squeezed the hard muscles on either side. This project had turned into so much more than getting revenge for Sebastian's suicide, and she was in way over her head.

Liam rubbed her back. "Are you okay, Katie-O? This is some pretty heavy stuff."

"I'll do what I can, Liam."

"You know why Sebastian died now. You know my agency is going to do everything in its power to put a stop to Tempest's activities." He stroked her hair. "You've done enough. We never would've had this intel if you hadn't been snooping around Garrett Patterson's office, putting yourself in danger. You can go home now, Katie."

She tilted her head. "Do you really think Mr. Romo and his sidekick are going to allow me to leave now? I'm part of their inner circle. They own me."

The corner of his mouth twitched. "They don't own Katie O'Keefe *or* KC Locke. Nobody owns either of those women."

"I'm not leaving here without you. So whenever you're done, I reckon that's when I'll wrap up."

He tugged on a lock of her hair. "Stubborn girl."

"You'd better get back. You can finish up when you return to the classroom, as long as nobody can see what you're doing. I can erase every trace of every keystroke."

"I think I can manage, but let's look up one more date here—one in the future."

The first location they searched for brought up another street, this time in Berlin. She jotted it down. "I'll search for any notable people at this address when I get home."

"There are only three more, all in the future. Do the last one on Patterson's list, and we'll call it a day." He closed his eyes and retrieved the coordinates.

She entered the numbers, and the location flashed onto the screen. She didn't need to look up this address or the occupants or the date.

It was the White House.

Chapter Twelve

The tap on the door made him jump from his chair, his adrenaline still coursing through his system after their discovery. He righted the chair as Katie called out, "Yes?"

Mills poked his head into the room. "Are you done in here yet, Ms. Locke? The recruits have lunch and psych."

Liam's stomach dropped. This new psych session had been slipped in at the last minute, thanks to Dustin. He had a feeling they were in for some heavy-duty hypnosis and probably another shot of T-101. Their loyalty had to be secured.

"I'm not quite done, but I can finish up what I'm doing without Mr. McCabe's help."

Mills worked his jaw back and forth before the words spilled from his mouth. "The recruits aren't supposed to allow their laptops out of their sight when they're not locked up in the classrooms."

Katie stopped tapping away on the keyboard and let her gaze travel up and down Mills's body. "I'm here on business for Mr. Romo. If you care to call him and verify, I'll be happy to wait."

Mills flushed up to the roots of his buzz cut. "I don't want to bother Mr. Romo. When you're finished, please return Mr. McCabe's laptop to the classroom. I'll be waiting for you so I can lock up."

"Will do." She flicked a glance at Liam. "Thank you for your cooperation, Mr. McCabe."

"You're welcome. Thanks for making my laptop faster."

"We'll see about that. I'll check in on your progress in a day or two."

"Got it." He gave her a mock salute and followed Mills out of the room and back into the classroom to retrieve his backpack and assignments.

Mills dropped into his chair and blotted his forehead with a tissue. "Between me and you, McCabe, that Ms. Locke is another Ginger Spann."

"You think? She seemed nice enough."

"Cold, bossy, just like Spann. She's definitely Romo's type, if you know what I mean—physically and every other way. He likes the tall, slender women, brainy types."

Liam almost tripped to a stop at the door. Gripping the doorknob, he twisted his head over his shoulder. "I don't know what you mean."

"You didn't hear it from me, but Romo and Spann are an item to put it politely, and I wouldn't be surprised if he had Ms. Locke lined up as a younger, newer model."

Liam lifted his stiff shoulders. "As long as it doesn't affect me."

"Yeah, not you guys." Mills's features had twisted into a sneer. "But when Romo sets up one of his lady friends, he gives her carte blanche over the rest of us. It's highly illegal on all levels—bed the boss and get all kinds of perks."

Liam's blood simmered, but he pasted on a smile. "Not my business."

Mills shook his head and blinked as if coming out of a rage-induced trance. "Of course not. Not mine, either. Just blowing off a little steam—just between us, eh, McCabe?"

Everyone around here walked on eggshells, afraid of retribution from Romo. Mills had let his anger loosen his tongue.

"Sure, Mills. Like I said, it's not my concern."

He walked back to his room, his mind racing. Had Katie not noticed Romo's attention, or had she just neglected to tell him about it? Maybe Mills just didn't like female authority. Katie had nettled him, and nobody liked Ginger Spann, so Mills was attributing their power to sleeping with the boss.

He had to put his concern for Katie on the back burner for now. She could handle Romo's advances. He had to get to his phone and deliver this new info to Prospero, whether or not he got reamed by his Prospero bosses for sneaking a phone onto the facility. This information couldn't wait. If Prospero could tie Tempest's agents to these other assassinations, they'd have a good case to make with the CIA for shutting down Tempest completely and revoking its funding.

He hung his backpack on the chair and washed his hands. Maybe he'd have some time after lunch and before the psych session to dig up his phone.

Lunchtime was buzzing with more talk of Dustin. To prove their superior insight, most of the recruits were now insisting they suspected something fishy about the guy. Liam kept his mouth shut.

Dustin had been using the cigarettes as an excuse for being in locations where he had no business being. How soon had he caught on to Tempest's true intentions? It had to have been before the T-101 injection, but that was probably the icing on the cake.

Would they be subjected to another dose this afternoon? A light sweat broke out on his skin. The docs at Prospero had no idea how long the T-101 antidote would work. Would there come a time when the formula would find an accepting host in his body? Then what? Would that be enough to compel a decent man to launch an attack against his own country?

"That leaves the field free and clear for McCabe."

"Huh?" Liam looked up from his turkey sandwich into the eager eyes of Charlie Beck.

"Gantt was the only one who could challenge you during PT. You're going to be the top dog now, free and clear, no challengers."

Not once they all got pumped up with T-101.

"I guess Gantt's body was a lot more fit than his mind."

"Yeah, yeah. He must've been nuts, right? Why else would he go out that way?" Charlie's voice carried an edge of hysteria that he probably didn't even notice.

Was he having his own doubts? Liam's gaze darted among the faces at his lunch table, and the smiles seemed tight and strained, the jaws tense. Were they all getting it now?

It would make his job a whole lot easier when it came time to roll.

He picked up his plate. "I'm going to try to squeeze in some fresh air before the psych sessions start, clear my mind."

Tammy, the lone female recruit, nodded toward the cafeteria door where one of the Tempest security guards stood with his arms crossed. "I think you're going to have a problem with that."

A few of the recruits at the table murmured. "Are they locking us in now? Damn Gantt."

Liam stacked his plate on a tray by the door and approached the security guard. "I'm done. Can you step aside?"

"Mr. Moffitt wants to make sure all recruits are in the waiting room by one o'clock."

Moffitt was the assistant to Hamilton, the physical trainer. Liam tapped his watch. "It's twelve-forty. I'm just going to get some fresh air."

The security guard's eyes slid from Liam's face to

the table of restless recruits behind him. "Yeah, sure, of course."

He stepped aside, and as Liam strode away from the cafeteria, he heard the guy get on his cell.

Liam made it to the track without seeing another soul, and then suddenly two figures emerged from the buildings on the other side of the facility. As they drew closer, Liam could make out their security guard uniforms and their equipment belts. Tempest believed in arming its security guards with more than pepper spray and a pair of zip-tie handcuffs.

So he was allowed to get his fresh air, but not without an escort. He could forget about calling Prospero on the phone, buried in the dirt on the other side of the track.

For show, he walked around the track, anyway, while the security guards stationed themselves on either end of it. Did they expect him to jump the fence and make a run for it toward the kiosk at the entrance to the facility? Gantt must've slipped through the gates when the fire trucks were on their way in to respond to the blast.

He and Katie would have to manage their own way out. He wouldn't be leaving her behind—not this time.

After making a point of walking around the track a few times and staring at the sky, Liam returned to the recruit facility and the claustrophobic waiting room, where even Charlie wasn't playing video games.

The mood had changed for the recruits. Gantt's escape had planted ideas in their heads, ideas that they'd dismissed before as preposterous.

Did they finally understand that they couldn't leave at this point of their own free will? Couldn't break their contracts? They'd owe Tempest money back from their signing bonuses, but Gantt must've realized that wouldn't be the only consequence of his defection.

Mr. Romo had to be aware of the rumblings, and he'd

Send For
2 FREE BOOKS
Today!

I accept your offer!

Please send me two
free novels and two mystery
gifts (gifts worth about $10).
I understand that these books
are completely free—even
the shipping and handling will
be paid—and I am under no
obligation to purchase anything,
ever, as explained on the back
of this card.

❏ I prefer the regular-print edition
182/382 HDL GJCE

❏ I prefer the larger-print edition
199/399 HDL GJCE

Please Print

FIRST NAME

LAST NAME

ADDRESS

APT.#   CITY

STATE/PROV.   ZIP/POSTAL CODE

Visit us online at
www.ReaderService.com

© 2015 HARLEQUIN ENTERPRISES LIMITED. ® and ™ are trademarks owned and used by the trademark owner and/or its licensee. Printed in the U.S.A.

▲ Detach card and mail today! No stamp needed. ▲

Send For
2 FREE BOOKS
Today!

I accept your offer!

Please send me two free novels and two mystery gifts (gifts worth about $10). I understand that these books are completely free—even the shipping and handling will be paid—and I am under no obligation to purchase anything, ever, as explained on the back of this card.

❏ I prefer the regular-print edition
182/382 HDL GJCE

❏ I prefer the larger-print edition
199/399 HDL GJCE

Please Print

FIRST NAME

LAST NAME

ADDRESS

APT.#   CITY

STATE/PROV.   ZIP/POSTAL CODE

Visit us online at
www.ReaderService.com

I-815-GF15

© 2015 HARLEQUIN ENTERPRISES LIMITED. ® and ™ are trademarks owned and used by the trademark owner and/or its licensee. Printed in the U.S.A.

▲ Detach card and mail today. No stamp needed.

take action. It would push up the schedule for indoctrination. Once Tempest had thoroughly drugged and brainwashed the recruits, they wouldn't want to leave. They'd be tied to Tempest for life. The only way out—suicide, like Sebastian and Adam, total, crazed rebellion like a previous agent, Simon Skinner, or escape like Max Duvall from whom Prospero had gotten the bulk of their intel.

He nodded at a couple of the other guys and grabbed a sports magazine, burying his nose in the pages. He didn't want to talk to anyone. At this point he wouldn't put it past Tempest to monitor the recruits' every move. If they didn't trust him enough to get a breath of fresh air on his own, they must be in extreme paranoid lockdown mode.

Time to make a move, take what they had and get the hell outta Dodge.

The monitor opened the door and called in the first four recruits for their sessions. He'd just been bumped up the list, along with Charlie and Tammy. Again he was the last drop-off along the hallway and again Dr. Harris awaited him.

"Hello, Liam. Take a seat." She gestured toward the couch. The chair he'd occupied last time had been removed.

He sank on the end cushion of the couch, across from her chair. "You must want me to lie down this time since the chair is gone."

"You're very observant." She tapped the end of her pencil on her knee.

He spread his hands. "That's why I'm here. Spies are supposed to be observant, right?"

"You seem…hostile today."

"I suppose I don't like being tailed by a couple of security guards when I'm out for a walk."

"You understand what's going on."

"Dustin Gantt."

"That's right. He put lives in danger. We can't allow that to happen again."

"Understood." He snapped his fingers. "He wasn't your patient, was he? Mr. Romo's gonna wonder why one of his shrinks screwed up and didn't see the signs in Gantt."

One corner of her mouth lifted. "Don't worry about me. How'd the vitamin shot make you feel last time?"

"Good." He raised his eyes to the ceiling. "Strong. Sharp. Tempest should put that stuff out to the general market. They'd make a mint."

"It's reserved for our agents. Are you ready to go under again?"

"Sure, as long as you don't make me dance like a chicken."

"I did that last time."

He smacked his knee and rocked back on the couch in an enthusiastic show for the first glimmer of humor he'd seen from any of the Tempest drones.

Her lip turned up again in that half smile. "Let's get to work."

She tried the same trick on him with the eraser end of her pencil tick-tocking in front of his face. He imagined weights pulling at his lids and allowed them to droop over his eyes, all the while keeping his mind clear. Prospero had trained him well, not that he'd ever been susceptible to hypnosis.

When she believed he'd gone under, her questions and suggestions dealt with the recent past this time. She encouraged him to talk about Dustin Gantt, asking him his true feelings about Gantt and his escape. Did they really expect to get at any truths this way? Romo seemed to have an inordinate amount of faith in hypnosis.

He made sure to let his disgust of Gantt's actions seep into his narrative. He also revealed his encounter with Gantt near the parking structure just so he didn't come across as too perfect since he'd never reported that encounter.

Dr. Harris finished up her questions and brought him out of what she thought was his hypnotic state.

"How do you feel, Liam?"

"Good. Relaxed."

"Great. Are you ready to feel even better?"

"Another vitamin shot?"

"That's right." She twisted around and picked up her cell phone. "He's ready."

Liam's muscles tensed up. He hated this part—too many uncontrolled variables. Did that antidote have a long shelf life or did it wear off? The Prospero doctors hadn't had enough time to figure out much before he had to join the next Tempest recruitment.

A nurse walked through the door, pushing a cart in front of her. "Are you ready, Mr. McCabe?"

"As ready as I ever am for a needle poking me in the arm." He rolled up his sleeve.

The nurse shot a quick glance at Dr. Harris. "This time the injection is going into your buttocks. Sorry, but can you please stand, turn around and pull down your jeans and underwear?"

The pulse in his jaw ticked. "Ah, sure."

He pushed off the couch and turned to face the wall. *Why the change?*

He unbuttoned his fly, hooked his thumbs in the elastic band of his briefs and yanked down his pants and underwear.

She swabbed a spot on his right buttock. "This will sting a little."

He gritted his teeth as the syringe went into his flesh. He expected to feel no reaction, just like last time. What he got was a surge of adrenaline and darkness crowding his peripheral vision.

"Whoa." He swayed toward the couch and flung out his hand, which hit a picture on the wall.

The nurse grabbed his arm and eased him onto the couch, his pants and briefs still twisted around his thighs. "Just relax, Mr. McCabe."

"Is he going to be okay?" Dr. Harris hunched forward in her chair as he fought to focus on her face swimming before him.

From somewhere far away, he heard the nurse's voice. "I administered a double dose, just like you requested."

Chapter Thirteen

Katie took a deep breath and hugged her file folder to her chest as she waited next to the executive elevator. She'd been dreading this appointment all day, but she'd come prepared.

She'd had no contact with Liam since he'd left for lunch and another appointment with the psychiatrist. After Dustin Gantt's escape, Mr. Romo would be coming down hard on the recruits, but Liam had a plan in place. He'd told her nothing the psychiatrist did, including shooting him up with T-101, would have any effect on him.

The clip of Ginger's heels echoed down the corridor as she approached the elevator. She pushed her glasses on top of her head as she drew next to Katie and flashed her badge to call the elevator car. Lifting one sculpted, carefully groomed eyebrow, she glanced at the file folder. "Fruitful afternoon?"

"Absolutely." Katie raised her hand at a passing co-worker from programming, but the person looked away and scurried past the elevator.

Word had gotten out. She'd been lumped in with Ginger Spann. Mr. Romo had plucked her from the obscurity of the worker bees and had elevated her to the secret society of executive elevators and private afternoon meetings. It's what she'd hoped for, what she'd planned for once she figured out the lay of the land at Tempest, but it made her feel…unclean.

The doors whispered open, and Ginger gestured with her hand. "After you."

Katie retreated to a corner of the elevator, still gripping her folder and staring at the lighted numbers even though they would make only one stop.

"You're discreet, KC. I like that." Ginger touched a finger to her lips and stretched them into one of her stingy smiles.

"I have to be discreet. If it gets around that I'm digging into employees' computers, this operation would be a total failure."

"You enjoy it, don't you? You like the thrill of the forbidden." Ginger crossed her arms and wedged a shoulder against the mirrored wall.

"I admit it." Katie blew a lock of hair, which had escaped from her chignon, from her face. "I like solving other people's puzzles. That's what hacking is—solving a puzzle someone else put into place."

"But those computer programs are supposed to be impenetrable for a reason. Face it. You love breaking the rules." She shook a finger at her as the car landed on Mr. Romo's private floor. "You naughty girl."

"Rules are meant to be broken." Katie tossed her head, and her loose bun came undone in a shower of bobby pins.

"Exactly." Ginger's eyes lit up and Katie relaxed her shoulders, knowing she'd given the appropriate response— one that Ginger had been waiting for from her, one that had solidified her membership in the covert triumvirate.

As Katie ducked to retrieve the pins on the floor of the elevator, Ginger placed the toe of her shoe over one of them. "Leave them. Mr. Romo will like your hair like that."

Katie raised a flushed face to Ginger. "I—I don't, I'm not…"

Ginger patted her hot cheek. "Oh, I know you're not trying to seduce Mr. Romo, KC. Don't worry. That's not what he thinks, either."

Katie was about to blurt out that Mr. Romo was the creepy, sexual harasser in this triangle, but she pressed her lips into a thin line. If she wanted to keep this position and help Liam, she'd have to suck it up and make nice with Romo.

But she'd have to draw the line somewhere—wouldn't she? How far did spies go to secure their mole status? Did they ever sleep with the enemy?

There's only one man she wanted to sleep with right now, and he was somewhere on the other side of this facility getting his head shrunk.

Ginger rapped her knuckles on Mr. Romo's open door. "We're here for the three o'clock meeting."

"Wonderful." Mr. Romo rubbed his hands together, and even this seemingly innocent gesture had knots forming in Katie's gut.

He stood up and gestured to the chair across from his regular spot on the couch.

Without waiting for an invitation, Ginger sat on the other end of the couch, crossing one long leg over the other.

Katie perched on the edge of the chair, resting the manila folder on her knees, her muscles coiled. She didn't want either one of them taking her by surprise.

Mr. Romo picked a piece of lint from the lapel of his dark jacket. "What did you find out about Dustin Gantt, KC?"

Katie flipped open the folder and positioned her index finger on the first bogus bullet point she'd created for Gantt.

"Well, if you had any lingering doubt that Gantt was responsible for the explosion, his browsing history should dispel it." She tapped the page. "He'd done a little research on gas lines. He'd also found a map of the facility."

Mr. Romo leaned back, lacing his hands behind his neck. "Good, good. Did he have any contacts on the outside?"

"No. I found one email account belonging to him with one of the free providers, but he'd followed instructions before arriving here and had deleted the account. There was no suspicious activity on that account before he reported to training."

"What about instant messaging with anyone within the company?" Ginger hunched forward. "Was he communicating with anyone? Samantha Van Alstyn?"

"Samantha?" Katie jerked her head up. "Why would Dustin Gantt be communicating with Samantha?"

Ginger's eye twitched. "She seemed overly interested in the recruits. You knew her. Didn't you notice that?"

"I think Samantha was overly interested in the recruits' hot bods, nothing more." She allowed her folder to slide off her knees as her mouth dropped open. "Oh, my God. You don't think Gantt had anything to do with Samantha's accident, do you?"

"How could he?" Mr. Romo had reached over, placing a hand on Ginger's thigh.

Was that a love tap or a warning to keep her mouth shut about Samantha?

Ginger cleared her throat. "Of course not. Gantt was still here when Samantha had her unfortunate accident, but perhaps Samantha was distraught over something Gantt mentioned to her."

"You're grasping at straws, Ginger. Samantha didn't know Dustin Gantt, and there's a way to trace deleted instant messages." The lie rolled off Katie's tongue. "Gantt had no instant messages other than to Mr. Mills regarding some classroom assignments, messages he never bothered to delete."

"Ahh." Mr. Romo tilted his head back and raised a fist in the air. "Isn't she magnificent, Ginger?"

"She is, indeed." Ginger dropped her hand to Mr. Romo's knee to mark her territory again. "What did you do about McCabe?"

"Do about him?"

Ginger tsked. "Don't let us down now, magnificent KC. Did you check out his computer?"

"Of course. I planted some tracking programs on his laptop so that I can monitor his keystrokes while he's in the classroom. You might be barking up the wrong tree there. I didn't note any unusual activity on his computer."

"Keep looking." Mr. Romo smoothed his thumb across the back of Ginger's hand. "Anything more to report on Gantt?"

"I'm still looking at him, too. In fact, I was going to ask you if it was okay if I took his laptop home with me tonight to do some work over the weekend."

Mr. Romo tilted his head at Ginger. "Does he have anything confidential on it?"

Ginger shook her head. "Frank, KC's boss, cleaned everything off just like he does for every employee who leaves."

"I can verify that." Katie held up her finger. "There's nothing on Gantt's computer except for his assignments."

With his unusual eyes crinkling at the corners, Mr. Romo said, "You are adorable, KC. No plans but work this weekend? A pretty girl like you?"

Nobody had ever called her adorable before. When she'd recovered from the shock, she peeled her folder from the floor. "Not a lot of socializing to be had in this town. I figured that's why Tempest chose this location—the dearth of distractions."

"We create our own social life." He winked at Ginger, who smiled like a sleek cat who'd just lapped up the last of the cream.

Katie held her breath, waiting for him to invite her into their social whirl. She didn't have to wait long.

"Any time you feel like joining us, just let Ginger know." He stood up and stretched his powerful frame. "No pressure. I know you're a little shy. Maybe you're more comfortable with computers than people."

She stood up and met his gaze at eye level. "Mr. Romo, I'm here to do a job, and I'm more than happy to help you in any way I can. I'm not really looking for...anything else."

Her muscles tensed, bracing for his anger. She shouldn't have challenged him, but wasn't that what a normal employee, under normal circumstances, would do when her boss started making inappropriate suggestions?

His lips twisted into a smile. "I appreciate your dedication to the job, KC. Come, let's have our group hug to reinforce our commitment to each other and to Tempest."

That wasn't too bad. Katie let out a measured breath and stepped in for the embrace. She could put up with this nonsense as long as Romo understood she wanted nothing more from him...or Ginger.

Ginger curled her arm around Katie's waist and drew her into the circle.

Mr. Romo placed his arm lower than Ginger's and tucked Katie against his side. His hand dropped to her backside, and he dug his fingers into her flesh beneath the gabardine of her slacks.

As she gasped, he pressed his forehead against the side of her head and growled. "You'll do whatever I want whenever I want it."

Then he stuffed his tongue in her ear.

KATIE CLUNG TO the toilet seat and retched for the third time. She staggered to her feet and hunched toward the mirror, staring into her red-rimmed eyes. "Sissy!"

She splashed cold water on her face and brushed her teeth. Then she flipped down the toilet seat and sat, digging her elbows into her knees.

A little tongue action from Romo and she'd collapsed like a tent in a windstorm. Of course, she'd waited until she got home for the complete breakdown.

In his office she'd blushed and stammered and pretended it's what she'd wanted from him all along, but claimed she didn't understand the situation since he seemed so close with Ginger.

They'd both gotten a big kick out of her naïveté, and Ginger assured her she wanted nothing more than for the three of them to form an intimate relationship. Katie pretended shock and insisted she needed time, and blah, blah, blah.

She didn't have to go far to convince either one of them since Romo seemed to think he was God's gift to womankind, and Ginger shared his assessment of himself.

She had discovered one thing—there's no way she could submit to Romo even for God and country. She'd have to get out of there before that eventuality took place.

And she had a plan, if only Liam would contact her. She figured he couldn't get to his phone. Post-Dustin, Tempest had the recruits under a microscope.

In the meantime, she had Dustin's laptop, and she intended to conduct a real investigation and find out where he went. Liam and his agency could use whatever info Dustin had dug up while a recruit.

She crept out of the bathroom and poured herself a glass of water. She still didn't even know if Tempest had her place bugged. It would give her some small satisfaction for

Mr. Romo to see the effect his attentions had on her, but she also knew it could be dangerous. *He* was dangerous.

He didn't just want people to work for him and do his bidding, he wanted his chosen employees completely under his control, sexually and every other way.

A tremble rolled through her body, and she shook it off. She sat cross-legged on her couch and pulled Dustin's computer into her lap and got to work.

She hadn't found any of that stuff on his computer that she'd reported to Mr. Romo and Ginger. She hadn't even checked his private email, but all recruits had been given explicit instructions to disable their accounts and not send or receive email while in training.

After a little investigating, it appeared that Dustin had followed orders—at least until he blew up the maintenance building. What had driven him to the conclusion that he'd have to escape or die at this point in his training? Had he recognized a kindred spirit in Liam and had tried to reach out to him? She'd probably ruined that moment between them at the parking structure.

She uncurled her legs and stretched them in front of her. A car alarm whined from somewhere outside, and she stopped short on her way to the kitchen. That car alarm belonged to her.

Stuffing her feet into a pair of clogs, she grabbed a jacket from the hook by the front door and swept her keys from the coffee table. She locked her door behind her and jogged downstairs to the parking garage beneath the building. The lights on her compact flashed as her alarm whooped it up.

She unlocked the car with her remote to stop the alarm and crept along the side of it, inspecting the windows. Had someone tried to break in to the vehicle? Her heart began to hammer almost as loudly as the alarm, and she glanced over her shoulder.

Her gaze darted to the dark corners of the garage where the overhead lights had burned out. She'd never noticed those missing lights before.

She locked her car and as she turned, an arm grabbed her around the waist, and a hand clamped over her mouth.

She bucked and raised her leg to stomp on her attacker's foot, just like Liam had taught her, but he blocked the move with his knee.

The man whispered in her ear. "Shh, shh. I'm not going to hurt you."

Relief flooded her body, and she slumped against Liam's chest. "Oh, my God. You scared the hell out of me. What are you doing out? Did you escape? Did something happen during the psych evaluation?"

Liam loosened his hold and turned her to face him with rough hands. He studied her through narrowed slits, his face a cold mask.

"Who the hell are you?"

Chapter Fourteen

The beginnings of Katie's smile froze on her lips. Her laugh gurgled to a stop in her throat.

Liam hadn't moved one taut muscle. His blue eyes glittered at her with a dangerous light.

"Stop messing around, Liam. I don't appreciate these kinds of jokes, especially after the day I had." She tried to jerk away from him but he held fast, his face, lined with confusion, inches from her own.

"Liam McCabe. I'm Liam McCabe."

Fear punched the words out of her. "Stop it. Just stop."

He tilted his head to the side as if deciphering a puzzle. "I know you. I had your address stamped in my memory. I had the make and model of your car stamped in my memory."

Full-blown panic coursed through her body. "What's wrong with you? It's me, Katie-O. God, don't play games with me, not now."

"I'm not playing games. Are you going to turn me in? Are you going to call someone to send me back to that place? I'm telling you straight up. I'm not going back."

"Liam, Liam." She pressed her palm against his unshaven cheek. "What happened? Don't you know me? I'm Katie O'Keefe. We're working together. We're…together."

Still holding her close with one arm, he dug his fingers into his left temple. "If you're lying to me, I'll…"

His eyelids flew open and he skewered her with his blue eyes, darker but eerily similar to Mr. Romo's—like there was nobody home.

She sobbed. "Please, Liam. I'm not lying to you. How did you escape from the facility? Why? Are they after you?"

His gaze tracked past her face, peering into the dark recesses of the garage. "Would they look for me here? It's the only address I knew, except for one in San Diego, and we're obviously not in San Diego."

She sniffed. "That's your home, *our* home. They're not going to look for you here, but they will look for you. How did you get out? Do they know you're missing?"

"I took out a security guard." He stepped back, and for the first time she saw his uniform. "He won't be discovered for a while."

"Good. Then you have time. What do you remember? You were fine this morning. We met. I talked to you."

"I need answers. I'm suffering from some kind of memory loss or amnesia. We can't stand in this garage all night. Is your place here or are you living with someone?"

"I live alone here, but we can't go up to my place. It might be bugged. You told me that, Liam."

"I need food or…something. I feel sick, agitated."

"It must've been the T-101. It got to you this time."

"T-101?"

She bunched the front of his shirt in her fists. "I know where we can go. There's a group of cabins not too far from here, close to the ski resort in Sun Valley. We'll rent one of those."

"Why can't we just drive, leave?" He'd clamped one hand on her shoulder.

He still didn't trust her.

"We can't. You'll understand why when I explain everything to you."

"If you try to take me back there…"

"You'll kill me." She put her fingers to his lips. "I don't plan on taking you back to Tempest."

"Tempest?"

Tears stung her nose and gathered at the back of her throat. She couldn't do this without Liam. Maybe he was right. Maybe they should just run. But the real Liam would never forgive her if she turned tail and took off when their work wasn't finished. He still had all those successful older brothers of his to live up to.

She squared her shoulders. "I'll explain everything." She unlocked the car. "Get in the backseat, on the floor. I'm going back up to my place to get my purse and throw a few things in a bag. It's Friday, and I'm going on a weekend getaway."

He finally released her and stepped back into the shadows. "I'll wait for you somewhere else."

She spun around and raced back to her apartment. She threw a few things into a suitcase and packed Dustin's laptop, along with her own. She dragged a blanket from her bed and then removed the floorboard in front of the fake fireplace and withdrew a bundle of cash, wrapping it in the blanket.

She'd learned a lot from Liam, and now it was her turn to teach him a thing or two.

FIFTEEN MINUTES LATER the woman—Katie—returned with a suitcase and her purse. Could he trust her? Every fiber of his being told him he could, but then he'd lost his memory so who could say he hadn't lost his gut instincts, too? But what choice did he have right now?

He had the security guard's gun, a little cash from the guy's wallet and numbers—addresses and telephone numbers and license plate numbers—dancing across his brain but not much else. As soon as Katie had said his name, he'd retrieved it. As soon as he'd seen her face, he'd recognized it.

All was not lost.

She whispered into the darkness. "Liam?"

He stepped forward from across the garage. "I'm here."

"Thank God. I thought you might've taken off."

"You're my lifeline, Katie, the only hope I have."

"Then get on the floor of the backseat. I have no idea if anyone's following me or watching me."

She'd popped the trunk of her car, and he lifted the lid for her and hoisted her suitcase in the back. Then he climbed into the backseat, and she threw a blanket in after him.

As she started the car, he folded his frame onto the floor. "You couldn't have found a bigger car?"

"Funny, you already asked me that once before."

She reached into the backseat and pulled the blanket over him. "That should help."

"How far away are these cabins?"

"An hour or so, not much more than that. Are you still hungry?"

His stomach growled. "Starving."

"I'll swing through a fast food drive-through once we get closer to the resort town. I don't want anyone asking questions about what I ordered and how much."

"Are you a spy, too?" He tucked the blanket around his frame, inhaling the scent of wildflowers that brought a rush of memories tumbling across his mind—kisses, soft skin, bodies melded together. Her body. No wonder he couldn't forget her.

She snorted. "I wasn't until fairly recently, but now I'm in a tangled web, and your memory loss has just tightened the noose."

"I'm not a complete blank slate. I do remember certain things—I know I'm a covert ops agent for Prospero."

"Propsero?"

His pulse quickened. "You don't recognize the name?"

"You never mentioned the name of your agency to me. I've never heard of it, but then I'd never heard of Tempest, either."

"Tempest—that's the place I escaped from."

"It's also a government agency. You were working undercover there for Prospero. Tempest is drugging its agents. You had an antidote, but something must've gone wrong this time."

His head pounded with the assault of information. "Okay, stop. Let me process this. You just drive."

She turned on the radio and tuned in to a country station. "This is for you. I prefer alternative rock and old punk."

He closed his eyes against the soft blanket and listened to the music as the car rocked back and forth. It was probably the first time he'd unclenched his jaw since the moment he'd woken up in that bed with no memory of who he was—just adrenaline coursing through his body and a sharp sense of danger.

He'd taken care of those two security guards as if they'd been ninety-eight-pound weaklings instead of two roided-out meatheads armed to the teeth. When he'd hopped the fence, he'd been able to clear it completely, avoiding the electrical field. With the address in town imprinted on his brain, he'd run the five miles to Katie's apartment building in record-setting time.

What the hell had happened to him?

After a while the car veered to the right, and Katie reduced her speed.

"Fast food ahead. It's a burger place. What do you want?"

"Everything."

The car bumped over the curb into a parking lot and slowed to an idle.

Katie buzzed down the window. "Three deluxe cheeseburgers with everything, two large fries, onion rings, chicken strips, two apple pies and a large vanilla shake, please. Oh, and a sugar-free lemonade."

The speaker gurgled something back, and she rolled forward.

He tucked the blanket around his shoulder in case the cashier decided to peek into the backseat of her car. "I hope you plan to share some of that with me."

"It's all for you. I'm a vegetarian."

"Of course you are."

She paid for the food at the next window. The rustle of paper bags and the smell of deep-fried everything made his stomach growl again.

The car lurched forward, took a few turns and accelerated uphill.

"We're almost there. Stay out of sight while I book the cabin. They're scattered along a hillside on the edge of a forest, so nobody will see us going inside. They're designed for privacy."

She parked, left the car and returned a short time later. "All set."

"Did you use a credit card?"

"I paid cash."

"Damn, you're good."

The tires crunched over gravel as Katie wheeled the car toward the cabin. "This is a nice spot. I saw these weeks ago when I was driving around one weekend."

The car stopped, and she opened the door. "I think we're good. Nobody's renting the next cabin over. I stressed that I wanted peace and quiet."

"That's exactly what I need right now." He threw off the blanket and rose stiffly from his cramped position half on the floor, half on the backseat. He staggered out of the car where Katie was already pulling her suitcase from the trunk, holding bags of food in the other hand.

"Let me get that." He took the suitcase from her and set it on the ground, looking at his surroundings. He took a deep breath of pine-scented air, crisp and cold. If anything could set him straight, this natural environment could do the trick.

Ducking back into the front seat, Katie grabbed the drinks from the cup holders. She hunched into her jacket and stomped toward the front door of the cabin. "It has a kitchen, too, so we don't have to go out for food, just groceries."

She pushed open the door and turned on a lamp, which bathed the room in a soft, yellow glow. "Rustic."

"Looks a lot better than the room I woke up in tonight."

Wedging her hands on her hips, she said, "I still don't understand how you got out of there."

He parked her suitcase in the corner of the room, next to the stone fireplace, and shrugged. "Super-human strength."

In the dim light of the cabin, Katie's face drained of all color.

"What's wrong?"

"It's the T-101. It got to you somehow."

"You mentioned that before. T-101 is some kind of formula Tempest is using? Why wouldn't it get to me?" He took the bags of food from her limp hand and placed them on the counter that separated the kitchen from the living room.

"You told me your agency—Prospero—had given you an antidote."

"I guess it didn't work." He ripped open the bag with

the cheeseburgers and sat on a stool at the counter. "Sit down and have a piece of lettuce."

"I see you're getting your bad sense of humor back. That has to be a good sign." She hopped onto the stool next to his and stuck her straw in the lemonade. "The thing is, the antidote *did* work, Liam. Today is not the first time Tempest administered it to the recruits."

"That's what we are, recruits? What are you doing there? Are you a recruit, too?"

"One question at a time. You eat and I'll explain." She puckered her lips around the straw and sucked up a sip.

He repositioned himself on the stool, damned glad that he and Katie were *together*, as she'd put it. He just didn't have the willpower to resist her charms, or was that the T-101 talking?

As he stuffed his face, she did a thorough job of explaining how they both ended up at Tempest, he working undercover for Prospero and she working under an assumed identity to investigate her friend's suicide.

If she glossed over answers to his questions about how they didn't realize each other would be at Tempest and how he didn't realize the Tempest agent who had killed himself was a mutual friend of theirs, he couldn't complain. He'd get the details later, or maybe his sieve of a mind would be able to fill them in. Things were shaping up more and more in his brain.

When she got to the part about Tempest's past and future assassinations, he tapped his head. "I still have those numbers right here. It may take me some time to make sense of them, but they're in my data bank."

"That's because you—" she dabbed something from his chin with the corner of a napkin "—are a freak of nature with a photographic memory."

Wrapping his finger around a strand of her wavy hair,

he pulled her face close to his. "It saved my life. It brought me to you."

Her dark lashes fluttered, and her plump lips curved into a smile.

He kissed that smile, slanting his mouth over hers. He slipped his hand behind her head, tangling his fingers in her thick hair and deepening the kiss. His erection throbbed and ached.

He could take her right now on top of this counter, on top of the remnants of his dinner. He drew her bottom lip into his mouth, between his teeth. She squeaked as he lifted her from her stool, pulling her between his legs, crushing her body against his.

Through the fog of his lust, he felt Katie's body, rigid and tense, not soft and compliant. He became aware of his hand yanking her hair and his thighs pinning her legs together.

He jerked back, blinking. "I'm sorry."

"I-it's okay." She put a shaky hand against his chest and then swept her tongue across a spot of blood on her bottom lip.

"My God, I hurt you." He jumped from the stool and grabbed a napkin from the counter. He soaked it with water and then leaned over the counter to dab her lip. "I don't always make love like a caveman, do I?"

A pink tide flooded her cheeks. "Sometimes, but you usually have a little more finesse than that."

"I know this is going to sound like some kind of lame excuse, but the T-101 made me do it."

"I believe you." She covered his hand with hers. "My lip's fine. Are you finished eating?"

"Yeah, and beginning to feel human again."

HE REALLY DIDN'T remember they'd called it quits. Was it so wrong to play house with him a little longer and reap the benefits? Although his advances had been a little rough, she had tingles in all the right places—and a few wrong places.

He started gathering the wrappers of his food and then twirled an onion ring around his finger. "Are you sure you don't want something? The rest of these onion rings? Some fries?"

She wrinkled her nose. "Most likely cooked in animal fat."

He chomped on the onion ring and raised his eyes to the ceiling. "Definitely animal fat."

"I had dinner before you set off my car alarm, anyway. I'm good." She rewrapped one of the burgers and put it in the fridge. Running her hands under the water, she asked, "So, you see why it's important that we stick around and finish the job."

"We need to try to destroy the facility and warn the other recruits, but I don't understand why you need to be involved anymore."

"Are you kidding me?" She grabbed a paper towel and dried her hands, turning to the side to watch him. "I guess you forgot that you'd started to put your faith in me that I could handle this job."

He closed his eyes and dug his fingers into his shoulder.

"Are you all right?" She stepped forward in case he toppled over, not that she could catch him but she could at least break his fall.

"Feels like I'm coming down from some incredible high." He pointed to the sink. "Can you get me a glass of water? Maybe I can flush this stuff out of my system."

"Is your memory returning?" She ran the water until it turned cold and filled a glass.

"Bits and pieces. I remember some of the recruits. I still don't remember the session that brought me here."

She handed him the glass, and their fingers brushed for

an electric instant. Their eyes clashed. Would he throw her on the counter like he'd obviously wanted to do ten minutes ago?

He took the glass and gulped down half of the water.

"I don't understand why the T-101 had that effect on you. It must be the antidote in your system. The other recruits got injected and it didn't affect them like you."

"Not that we know of." He downed the rest of the water, and she filled the glass again and handed it to him. "For all we know, the recruits are running amok."

"I wonder when they're going to find out you made your escape."

This time he sipped from the glass, watching her over the rim. "What's that going to mean for you if you return?"

"If?" She brushed stray strands of hair back from her face. "You mean *when*. I have to go back there, Liam. They have nothing to connect me with you other than the fact that they'd instructed me to spy on you. If I disappear now, my life will be in as great a danger as yours."

"And you don't think your life is in danger by returning to that hellhole?"

"I'm one of the chosen ones, the teacher's pet."

His jaw hardened. "What exactly does that mean? This Romo character sounds like a psycho. If he's not the brains behind Tempest, he's following orders like a good little psycho soldier."

"I can handle him." Her stomach twisted into knots as she mouthed the lie. She could no more handle Mr. Romo and his kinky desires than she could tell Liam the truth—that they were no longer a couple.

"Come here." He opened his arms and she went willingly, resting her cheek against his erratically pounding heart. "We have the weekend to think this through, right? By the end of that time, I will probably have regained most of my fleeting thoughts and shifting truths and can make some sense out of the whole mess."

She wrapped her arms around his waist and hugged him with all her strength. One weekend to pretend Liam McCabe was all hers again.

He kissed the top of her head. "Did the hotel clerk at the front desk say the fireplace was operational?"

"Not only operational, but there should be a cord of wood on the back porch and some kindling."

Tilting her head back with a finger beneath her chin, he brushed his lips across her mouth. "What are we waiting for?"

He released her and strode toward the back door off the kitchen.

She tossed the rest of the trash and wheeled her bag into the bigger of the two bedrooms. She'd snagged the smallest cabin—a two bedroom, one bath—but she had no intention of sending Liam to the other bed.

He called from the other room. "I got the wood. You okay?"

"I'm changing. I'll be right in."

"Wish I could change. Bring a couple of blankets with you."

She kicked off her clogs and peeled her jeans from her body. She pulled on a pair of black flannel pajama bottoms with pink lips on them and shimmied into a black camisole. Then she yanked a blanket off the queen-size bed and walked into the living room, dragging it behind her. She tripped over it when she saw Liam crouched in front of the fireplace, stoking the flames in nothing but his white briefs.

He cranked his head around. "I think this is going to work. Hurry up with that blanket. I had to get out of that polyester uniform, and now I'm cold."

"That's because you're half-naked." She draped the

blanket around her shoulders to cover her peaked nipples beneath her camisole—and her response had nothing to do with being cold. In fact, it had gotten extremely warm in here.

He stood up, the fire crackling behind him, his blond hair resembling a halo, and spread out his arms. "Nothing you haven't seen before, Katie-O."

"Do you remember calling me Katie-O, or is it just because I mentioned that nickname to you before?"

"Oh, I remember. I remember a lot of things." His slow smile ignited a flame in her belly. "Like that mermaid tattoo right above the sweetest spot in the world."

The flame licked at her insides, and the blanket dropped from her shoulders.

"Hey, we need that. I'm half-naked, remember?"

She swallowed. "How could I possibly forget?" Dipping down, she plucked up the blanket and walked as if in a trance toward Liam in his underwear.

He curled an arm around her and pulled her flush against his body, warmed by the fire. His erection bulged against his briefs, and she didn't know if it was the effects of the T-101 or her hand skimming between his powerful thighs.

He cupped her face with one hand and swiped his thumb across her throbbing lips, following up with a kiss. Then he stepped back and tugged on the blanket. "Is there another one of these in the bedroom?"

She swallowed as the cold air rushed between their bodies, raising goose bumps across her skin. Had he backed off because he was afraid the T-101 would turn him into an animal? Or had he just remembered that they hadn't been a couple at all because he'd left her?

"Yes. I'll get it."

"You stay here and warm up." He rubbed the gooseflesh on her arms. "I'll get it."

He brushed past her on his way to the bedroom, and she turned to admire the view of his broad shoulders tapering to a narrow waist and the thin cotton of his briefs clinging to his muscled buttocks. She just got warmed up.

She called after him. "What happened to your butt?"

He emerged from the bedroom with another blanket thrown over his shoulder. "What do you mean?"

"I saw the edge of a Band-Aid poking from the waistband of your underwear." She crouched down and spread out the first blanket on the floor over the throw rug.

"I have no idea." As he approached the fireplace, he dropped the other blanket and reached around to press his fingers against his backside. "Something happened because it's sore back there."

On her knees in front of the fireplace she patted the bed she'd made with the blanket. "Come on down here, and I'll have a look—if you insist."

The grin spread across his face as he joined her on the floor, stretching out and rolling onto his stomach, his tanned flesh at her fingertips. "I do insist."

She trailed her hand down the smooth skin of his back, her fingers making a detour around the scar on his side, courtesy of the Taliban. Hooking her fingers around the elastic of his briefs, she pulled them down, exposing the sculpted contours of his buttocks with one small plastic strip stuck to the top of the curve.

"What is it?"

"Hmm? What?"

He twisted his head around, his blue eyes smoldering beneath half-closed lids. "The Band-Aid. You're supposed to be looking at whatever's beneath it."

"Oh, I am." Her fingers played along the hard muscles of his backside, and she had the pleasure of watching him squirm. Then she picked at the edge of the plastic strip with her fingernail and peeled it back.

She sucked in a breath. "It's the site of an injection. It must be where they shot you up with T-101."

"Really?" He shifted to his side, propping his head up with one hand and stretching out his other arm. "Because last time, they shot me up in my shoulder. I still have that mark."

She rubbed the spot on his arm with two fingers. "Why would they change the injection site...unless the nurse just wanted you to drop trou?"

"Yeah, I have that effect on women."

"Watch yourself." She pinched his solid biceps and then sat up straight. "I got it—bigger muscle."

"Bigger injection."

"They'd decided to give you a higher dosage because the previous one didn't have the desired effect."

"This one didn't have the desired effect, either. Unless I ran around the track at the speed of light or lifted the corner of a small building before I collapsed on my bed, that extra dose was pretty much a waste of good T-101— until I took out their security guards and leaped over a tall, electrified fence."

"If you don't remember what happened, do you think they were able to question you?"

"I doubt it. I think the shot made me black out. If it didn't kill me, I don't think they expected me to wake up and escape."

She massaged his shoulder. "Thank God it didn't kill you."

"Thank God I didn't kill you."

"Since you had my address and license plate number emblazoned on your brain, it made sense that I was friend, not foe."

"I knew the second I wrapped my arm around you that you were friend." He turned his head and kissed the fingers that were prodding his shoulder. "In fact, I knew you were a lot more than friend. I could feel it in my...soul."

"You could tell that by cinching an arm around my waist and clapping your hand over my mouth?" She raised an eyebrow, but a thrill danced across her skin. They'd always had an electric current running between them, and she'd felt it again from the moment she bumped into him in the stairwell—two years apart vanished in a second.

"I could tell because my arm around you felt natural and right." He rose to his knees and dragged an ottoman in front of the fire. He leaned against it and tugged on her arm. "Join me, unless you're scared."

"Scared of what?" She crawled to his side, dragging the blanket with her, and settled next to him.

"Afraid of my Hercules-size strength and prowess." He draped an arm around her and tucked her against his body, where her head fell against his chest.

She stretched out her legs until her toes peeked from the bottom of the blanket. She wiggled them, luxuriating in the warmth of the fire and the feel of Liam's bare skin beneath her cheek.

"I told you before. You weren't hurting me and you didn't scare me."

"But this is nicer, huh?" He stroked her hair. "Slow and easy. It's been a while, and now we have all night."

"It hasn't been that long." She carefully threaded her fingers through his, holding her breath.

"Not that I can remember, but I'd have to bet we weren't getting it on in the hallways of Tempest, and from the looks of my room I wasn't a new arrival there."

She released a long breath. "I guess it has been a while."

"Let's not take it too slowly." He nudged her into his lap. "C'mon over here, woman."

She straddled him, placing her hands on his shoulders. "Are you sure you can handle it? I mean, just over two hours ago, you barely knew your own name and were threatening me with death."

"I'm feeling better with each passing minute. All that junk food and the water helped. The adrenaline has stopped pumping, and my head isn't so foggy."

"And the memories?"

"Slowly but surely. I should be fine by the end of the weekend."

"Then, what are we waiting for?" She twined her arms around his neck. If he'd wanted her as much as she'd wanted him, he'd forgive her this deception.

Tipping his head to the side, he kissed her throat. "You smell like wildflowers. You always smell like wildflowers."

"I roll around in them, naked." Her head fell back, and he buried his face in the crook of her neck.

"That I'd like to see, Katie-O." As he traced his tongue around the indentation in her throat, he slipped his fingers beneath the straps of her camisole. "Lift up your arms."

She obeyed, and he pulled the top over her head and tossed it over his shoulder onto the couch behind them. He cupped her breasts, circling her nipples with the pads of his thumbs.

She closed her eyes and parted her lips as she panted out his name. Rocking forward, she pressed her thighs against his erection.

A breath hissed out between his clenched teeth, and he sank his fingers into her hips, positioning her.

She looked into his face, and their eyes locked. Slipping a hand behind her neck, he pulled her close and kissed her—softly at first then with more and more urgency.

He shifted his body so that she slid off him. Then he wrapped his hands around her waist and pulled her down so that her back was flat against the floor.

"How are you still wearing pajama bottoms?"

"Probably for the same reason you're still wearing your underwear."

"On the count of three?"

She nodded, hooking her thumbs in the waistband of her pj bottoms.

"One, two, three."

She yanked off her bottoms and underwear in one flourish while Liam smiled down at her, his briefs still covering his essentials. She hit him over the head with her clothes. "Cheater."

He ran his hands down her body, placing his palms against her inner thighs. "I want this all about you for now."

She melted under his touch, and her legs fell open for him.

He positioned himself between her thighs and stroked her swollen flesh with the tip of his wet finger. His tongue followed, and she plowed her fingers through his hair, urging him on.

Since she'd already been fantasizing about Liam all week, the stroke of his tongue on her heated flesh sent her to dizzying heights within seconds. Her muscles tensed as all feeling centered in her core. One by one her worries melted away—Tempest's plans, Mr. Romo, Liam's memory loss. She let each one of them go.

They were back in San Diego, back when she'd been planning a life with someone for the first time ever, back before Liam had left her for another taste of honor and duty—one more scribble on the McCabe wall of pride.

He slipped his hands beneath her derriere and tipped her pelvis toward his exploring mouth.

The warmth invaded her body, seeping into her taut muscles and turning them to molten lava. Then the pleasure zigzagged through her body and when it tossed her from the precipice, she screamed her release.

As she rode out the remnants of her orgasm, Liam kissed her thighs, her belly, her breasts and took possession of her mouth and kissed her until she'd dissolved into a quivering puddle of goo.

He smiled against her lips. "I do remember that scream."

She sucked in his bottom lip. "You're not exactly quiet yourself."

"I don't remember at all. You're going to have to show me."

"I think I can do that—" she bucked him off her body and tapped her fingers along his rock-hard shaft "—big boy."

She scooted down the length of his body and took him into her mouth. She cupped his backside, skimming her fingernails across his skin.

He moved against her, in and out, his hands fisting in her hair. When she had his head thrashing from side to side, he jerked away from her.

"You're making me crazy. Let's put an end to this slow and easy stuff. I need to be inside you…now."

She kissed the side of his hip. "I was thinking the same thing."

He flipped her onto her back, and she didn't even need the fire anymore to stay warm. She was burning up.

He entered her in one smooth movement, filling her up and claiming her for his own. She hooked her legs around his thighs and he plunged deeper. He wouldn't last long enough to make her come again, and then suddenly he shifted his position until he was rubbing against all the right bits.

Had he known this trick two years ago?

Hot coils tightened in her belly, and her breasts ached as she clenched her jaw, ready for the explosion. It came. She came.

He came.

He growled just like a caveman as he drove into her, lifting her bottom from the blanket they'd spread beneath them.

Throwing back his head, he moaned as he spent himself completely.

"Shh." She smoothed back the hair from his damp forehead. "You're going to wake the bears."

He kissed her nose and her ear and then rolled to his side, yanking the blanket over both of them. "Whatever happens at Tempest, this night was well worth the price... and we're not done yet."

She stretched and yawned like a very satisfied cat. "I'm going to brush my teeth and get some water. You?"

"Same. Let's move this party to the bedroom. I'll see about the fire."

About fifteen minutes later they slipped between the sheets of the bed, and Katie snuggled against Liam's side. Maybe this had all been a huge mistake. How could she ever let this man out of her life again after this night?

Would she have a choice?

He'd left her before to join his navy SEAL team on a mission to free a doctor who'd been imprisoned for helping the US Forces. Now he and his Prospero team had to save the White House. What chance did her love have in the face of that calling? And did she even have the right to expect him to give up the calling?

She sighed and burrowed her head against his shoulder.

His breathing had deepened, and his chest rose and fell with every breath. He murmured something in his sleep.

He'd lied. He'd fallen into an exhausted sleep and not even another shot of T-101 could rouse him. They were finished...for now. And that was okay. She just wanted to drift off in the protection of his arms.

The next morning she awoke with a start. As she rubbed

her eyes, Liam's handsome face came into focus. He'd been watching her sleep.

She brushed her knuckles across the hard plates of his pectoral muscles and the light dusting of hair scattered across them. "It's heaven to see your face first thing in the morning. It's been a while, and I missed it. I missed you."

He quirked one eyebrow and trapped her fingers in his hand.

"Katie O'Keefe, you're a stone-cold liar."

Chapter Fifteen

She woke up fast. Her eyebrows shot up and she tried to snatch her hand away from his, but he had a tight grip.

"What do you mean?"

She managed a convincing tone, but the two red flags on her cheeks gave her away.

In one quick move that would do any juiced-up Tempest agent proud, he'd rolled her onto her back and straddled her hips, pinning her with his thighs. "We were not together before your infiltration of Tempest and hadn't been together for about two years."

She gulped, her Adam's apple bobbing in her delicate throat. "You understand why I had to tell that little lie, right?"

"Enlighten me."

"You had no memory. You'd just escaped from a situation you didn't completely understand, and you knew my address. You didn't know who I was. I could've been the enemy. I diffused the situation the fastest way I knew how."

Cocking his head, he studied her face. "You could've just told me we were friends or even exes—the truth."

"A friend doesn't carry the same emotional weight as a lover, and why would I tell you we were exes? That would give you even more reason to distrust me. Is the interrogation over now?" She bucked her hips to dislodge him and it only made him hard.

He clamped down on his bottom lip but didn't budge. "Kind of sadistic lying to some poor SOB who'd lost his memory, don't you think?"

"I did it for your own good." She gave up the struggle to get him off her, crossing her arms behind her head. "I'm glad your memory returned and that you're feeling better. You can sleep in the other bed tonight."

"Is that what you think I want?" He traced a finger from her pouting lips, down her neck, between her heaving breasts, along her flat belly and then outlined her mermaid tattoo.

She squirmed at his touch. "You called me a liar."

His fingers dabbled back up to her breasts, and he tweaked her nipple. "You are."

She squeaked. "Then if I'm such a big, fat liar, you can sleep in the other bed, away from my big, fat lies."

"Did you hear me complaining about your lies?" He rose to his knees, his erection protruding in front of him. He brushed the tip along her skin, and she closed her eyes and gripped the iron bars of the headboard above her.

"No," she whispered.

"Turns out, I kinda like the lie, and I really like that you used it to get me into bed."

Her lids flew open. "I did not…exactly."

He hovered over her face and nibbled on her earlobe. "Turn over."

Still trapped between his legs, she struggled to roll onto her stomach. He helped her and then brushed the hair away from her cheek so he could see her face, flushed with desire, her eyes half-closed. She curled her fingers around the bars of the headboard again, and he pressed his lips against the corner of her mouth.

Then he laid a trail of kisses from the nape of her neck,

down her back and along one creamy cheek of her luscious derriere. Hooking an arm around her waist, he hoisted her up to her knees and entered her from behind.

Having her wrapped around him felt just like coming home. Her body moved with his, accepting every inch of him. He reached around and stroked the moist folds of her flesh, close to where their bodies were joined together.

She arched her back and then exploded around him. He continued to drive into her as she quaked and trembled on her knees. His release came hard and jagged, ripping a cry from his throat.

He folded on top of her, and she collapsed beneath him. He kept moving against her, the soft flesh of her backside pressing against his thighs, keeping the fire burning in his belly.

He didn't want to go back to his world—didn't give a damn about Tempest, didn't want to return to Prospero, didn't care what his brothers thought of him—just wanted to drown in the pleasures of this woman.

"You're crushing me." She wriggled beneath him, and he hardened once more inside her.

He couldn't blame the T-101 for that. He turned onto his side, taking her with him, still maintaining their connection, spooning against her back. He cupped her breasts and toyed with her nipples.

"Is this my punishment for lying?" She captured his hand and pulled it down between her legs. Using his fingers, she traced along the seam that joined their bodies.

He undulated his hips, growing inside her, and she moaned, soft and low. He could take her again, right now.

The ringing of Katie's cell phone on the nightstand shattered the heavy sensuality that had encompassed the bed... and his brain.

Katie made no move toward her phone, instead taking one of his fingers and using it to pleasure herself again.

But the insistent ringing had brought him back to reality. He pulled away from her, out of her, dousing cold water on their hot emotions. "You need to get that."

By the time she'd come out of her haze and fumbled for the phone, it had stopped ringing.

"Who was it?"

She squinted at the cell, sucked in a breath and then turned the display toward him.

He read the words with dread beating against his temples. "Ginger Spann."

"They know." She dropped the phone as if it were contagious. "They know by now that you escaped and that has to be why she's calling me. She wouldn't call me on a Saturday unless it was urgent."

He picked up the phone with two fingers and swung it in front of her face. "Then you'd better call back."

"Do you think they'll ping my phone to find out where I am?" She dragged the sheet up to her chin and stared at him over the edge with round, bright eyes.

"They might, but they definitely will if you ignore Ginger's call." He tapped the phone against his chin. "You took the weekend to get away from it all. They already think you're some sort of computer geek, right? It shouldn't be a stretch for them to think you took off on your own. Offer to come back in the office if they need you."

"I thought you didn't want me going back there."

"I don't. They're not going to make you come back. Anything you can do at this point you can do remotely, but make the offer, anyway." He squeezed her shoulder. "Are you ready?"

She nodded and tapped Ginger's name before putting the phone on speaker. It rang once before Ginger picked up.

"KC, thanks for calling back so quickly."

"I was in the shower. What do you need, Ginger?"

"Another recruit left the facility—Liam McCabe."

Katie gasped. "You and Mr. Romo were right about both of them—Gantt and McCabe. How did you know? I saw nothing in McCabe's computer usage."

"It was something else, something I can't tell you about, KC."

"I understand completely, Ginger."

Katie's obsequious, butt-kissing tone made him sick to his stomach. Who knew his computer-hacker girl had such amazing acting chops?

"Obviously, you didn't see him wandering around the town or anything, or you would've called us...right?"

"Wandering around the town? Why would a recruit escaping from the facility be wandering around the next town over, waiting to be discovered?"

"We have reason to believe McCabe is not in his right mind."

"How did he escape? I thought we were watching the recruits after Gantt's stunt."

That use of *we* was a nice touch. He smiled at Katie and nodded.

"He... I can't tell you that, either, KC."

"Did he hurt anyone? Is everyone okay? Mr. Romo?"

Liam rolled his eyes.

"He did hurt people. He's a dangerous man, but Mr. Romo is fine."

"Have you called the authorities?"

"Yes, yes, of course we notified the police."

Liam mouthed to Katie, *Liar*. Tempest would never bring the local authorities into its business.

"Do you want me to come in, Ginger? Is there anything I can do to help?"

"No need. I just wanted to warn you, give you a heads-up, and if you're still working with Gantt's computer, dig deeper and see if you can find a connection between him and McCabe."

"I definitely will and if you change your mind—I'm there."

Liam held his breath. She'd almost reached the finish line and Ginger hadn't asked her about her location.

"So sweet of you to offer, KC, especially after the little incident in Mr. Romo's office yesterday."

Liam jerked his head up, drawing his brows over his nose. Katie hadn't mentioned an incident, but then he hadn't given her much time.

She glanced at Liam, her face reddening. "Oh, it was just a misunderstanding."

"Mr. Romo has…particular tastes, and he deserves to be indulged. I do indulge him, KC. He had his eye on you from the moment you arrived at Tempest and had instructed me to find out what you could do to help us. That's the main reason we brought you in—he knew you were special."

A dull pain throbbed at the base of Liam's skull. What the hell kind of particular tastes was Ginger going on about? Katie would not meet his eyes. It had to be bad.

Katie rushed her words. "My talents matched up with what you needed, so it worked out for everyone."

"We're glad to have you in our inner circle. *I'm* glad to have you, so don't ever worry about making me jealous. There is no room for jealousy between me and Mr. Romo. I hope that eases your mind and you're willing to relax and enjoy what Mr. Romo has in store for you."

"I—I'm sure I will, Ginger. It's like I told you…"

"I know. You're shy, you're unsure of yourself. Mr. Romo saw that in you, and he's eager to awaken you. He'll set free your desire to serve. You'll get immense pleasure from catering to Mr. Romo's needs."

Liam curled his hands into fists and punched the pillow on his lap. Through a fog of rage, he only half listened to Katie ending the call through her blushes and stammers.

She paused for a long time and then looked up with a half-smile. "At least she didn't ask where I was."

"How long has that stuff been going on, how far has it gotten and why didn't you tell me about it?"

"It just started, really, and you had enough to worry about."

"Damn it, Katie." He chucked the pillow across the room. "You cannot go back there. You don't know what Romo is capable of. He might even drug you. He probably uses T-101 himself to keep up with his particular tastes, as Ginger politely put it."

"I think I'm safe for now. Mr. Romo has his hands full with Gantt's defection and now yours."

"Yeah, I know what he wants his hands full of, and stop calling him *Mr.* Romo like you have some kind of respect for him."

"I can't think of him any other way. I figured Ginger called him Mr. Romo even when they were between the sheets." She punched him in the arm.

"You're making jokes about those two in bed?"

She tilted her head, gathering her messy hair in one hand. "You act like that's worse than what they've already done and what they have planned for the White House— whatever that is."

"And you're acting like it's nothing at all." He grabbed her hand. "Don't put on the tough act with me, Katie. Romo is a dangerous character."

"I know that, Liam. That's why we need to put him out of business." She squeezed his fingers. "I'm not a recruit. I can come and go as I please."

"For now. Do you really think Ginger Spann has any freedom?"

"She doesn't want freedom from Mr.—from Romo."

"Maybe not now, but we don't know what happened to

make her this way. Who knows? Maybe she was a sweet, shy little geek at one point, too."

"Let's talk about this later. I'm starving." She leaned forward and kissed him full on the mouth. "I'm going to shower first if you don't mind. Then I'm going to run out for groceries. I think it's best if you stay hidden for now, don't you?"

"Probably. Do you think there's a clothing store in town?"

"There are a couple of ski runs here. Even though they're not open yet, I'm sure the town has clothing stores. Write down your sizes for me."

"Get me a baseball cap and some sunglasses, too, something I can use as a disguise."

She stumbled off the bed, dragging the sheet with her. "So, when did you recover your memory and do you have all of it back?"

"I started regaining bits and pieces last night. The food helped, the water helped, the sex helped a lot."

Her hands outlined a circle in the air. "I mean all of it. When did you remember we'd split up?"

"This morning when I woke up." He told her the lie with a straight face. In fact, he'd remembered how stupid he'd been two years ago as soon as he'd taken her into his arms in front of the fire.

And he had no intention of repeating his stupidity. He'd never let this woman go again even if it meant he'd failed in his mission for Prospero. He could handle failure. He couldn't handle losing Katie again.

KATIE FACED THE warm spray, massaging the soapy washcloth over her body, parts of it still sensitive from Liam's touch. He'd reclaimed her with...vigor.

She felt a petty sense of pleasure about his jealousy over Mr. Romo. Sure, the man was lethal, but having some kind of relationship with him was about the least lethal position he could take. In fact, any true spy worth her salt would take Mr. Romo up on the offer and strike when he was at his most vulnerable.

Not that she planned to suggest this to Liam. He'd go ballistic. Her lips curved into a smile as she splashed water on her face.

But she still needed to get back to work. She had a facility to shut down, and Liam needed to warn the other recruits and set them free from their bonds.

He'd infiltrated Tempest for Prospero, not only to get intel, but to hamper their operations and interfere with the flow of agents out of the academy. The agency had already executed several successful hits, and the CIA had never suspected the complicity of Tempest agents in those assassinations.

She and Liam had a chance to seriously damage Tempest's operations. She wanted to do it for Sebastian, for Samantha and for all those other agents.

She ended her shower and pulled on a pair of jeans and a black sweater. She planned to burn all of her slacks, blouses and low heels when she escaped from Tempest.

She picked up a pair of black motorcycle boots and walked to the living room where Liam had built up the fire again.

He turned around and leveled a finger at her. "Now that's the Katie-O I remember—tight jeans, lots of black and boots. All you're missing is the dark purple nail polish and black eyeliner."

"No point in putting on the nail polish only to remove it by Monday." She dropped to the ottoman and pulled on her right boot. "I'll be happy to see you out of that uniform."

He winked. "You already did."

"You have a dirty mind, McCabe."

He chuckled. "I wrote down a list of clothes and sizes, if you can find them."

"I'll do my best. Are you going to call Prospero?"

"To report my failure?"

"I'd hardly call what you achieved a failure. You got on the inside, identified the other recruits and decoded Patterson's notes. We're still going to bring down the facility."

"Not at the expense of your safety."

She put on her other boot and stomped her feet. "You didn't invite me along on this operation. I came on my own. You do what you need to do, and I'll do what I need to do. So, you're not calling Prospero?"

"I don't have a phone, and I'm not using yours to call in."

"I can try to pick up a disposable."

"It's on the list." He crossed the room to the kitchen, grabbed a piece of white paper and waved it at her. "I'm way ahead of you."

"That's why you're the spy and I'm not."

"You could've fooled me. You're doing a helluva job so far."

She snatched the list from his hand and stood on her tiptoes to kiss him. "Can you hold out until I get back?"

He slipped a hand beneath her black sweater and caressed her breast through her bra. "For this?"

"One track mind. You sure that T-101 is out of your system? I meant, can you wait for food?"

"I can always eat the leftover burger in the fridge." He pulled her into his arms. "Be careful out there, Katie-O."

As she drove away, she saw the curtain at the window fall into place. She'd been counting on Liam's help for her plan to shut down Tempest, but he couldn't step foot on the place now. They'd figure out something. She refused to leave this alone and walk away now.

Driving the two miles into town, she kept one eye on

her rearview mirror. Ginger had given no indication that she suspected her of being out of town, but Elk Crossing was too close to the Tempest facility for comfort.

She made her first stop at a clothing store where she managed to find a pair of jeans, some long-sleeved T-shirts and a flannel shirt. She picked out a baseball cap with an elk on it and a black stocking cap that could be pulled down to mask the face.

She ducked into a ski shop for a scarf and a pair of sunglasses, but not even the convenience store had a disposable cell phone. Then she hit the grocery store and bought enough food for a couple of breakfasts, lunches and dinners. They didn't need to go out to any local restaurants. There weren't enough people in town yet to be inconspicuous.

She loaded the grocery bags into the trunk and tucked the clothes in between the bags.

She slid into the front seat and as she reached for the ignition, she heard a different kind of click next to her ear.

"You make one false move and I'll blow your head off."

Chapter Sixteen

Her heart galloped in her chest as she gulped for air, staring straight ahead. She didn't dare look in her rearview mirror in case he offed her for being able to ID him. On the off chance she had a run-of-the-mill criminal in her backseat, she stammered. "T-take my purse. Take my car. I haven't seen you, and I'm not interested in seeing you."

"I don't want either of those things, although the car might come in handy later. And I don't give a damn if you see me or not."

She shifted her gaze to the mirror and her mouth dropped open. "Dustin Gantt."

"The one and only. Now take me back to that little love nest you're sharing with McCabe."

Her nostrils flared. "I don't know what you're talking about."

"Drop it. I tracked your car there. I saw you from the woods."

"How?"

He hunched his shoulders. "I didn't leave Tempest empty-handed."

"What do you want from us? We're on the same side." She felt like banging her head against the steering wheel. She'd been so cocky and sure of herself, and she'd failed Liam.

"Maybe, maybe not. I want answers."

"Then get that gun away from my head, or I'll have to assume you're working for Tempest."

He practically growled. "After what those people did to me? They're lucky I didn't blow up the whole damned place."

"You didn't want to kill anybody. That's why you hit the utility building."

He grunted. "I wouldn't say that. I just didn't want to kill anyone who didn't deserve it—and there are plenty there that do."

He lowered his weapon and she released a long breath. "Thank you. Liam wanted to find you, and now you've found us."

"Why'd he want to find me?"

"He figured you'd discovered something about Tempest, and he wanted to pick your brain. We really are on your side."

"Then take me back to that cabin."

"I need to tell Liam first."

"No!" He waved the gun again and she instinctively ducked. "Why do you think I didn't approach you at the cabin when I had the chance? McCabe is lethal. But now you're my insurance. I don't know what game you two are playing, but I'm not taking any chances until I find out. And if you don't take me with you, I guess I'll make an anonymous call to Tempest, because if McCabe is here with you, chances are Tempest would be very interested in that piece of news."

"Okay. I'll take you to the cabin."

"Don't try anything stupid, Ms. Locke. Just because I'm not pointing my gun at you doesn't mean I can't remedy that situation in about a half a second."

She licked her dry lips. "I believe you."

She maneuvered the car back on the winding road to the cabin. As the manager's cabin came into view, she said,

"Get down in the backseat. For all the manager knows, I arrived here alone, and he doesn't need to know anything else."

Gantt slid down in the seat as she drove the back road to the cabin. Wouldn't Liam be surprised?

She screeched to a stop in a hail of gravel and dust in front of the cabin.

Gantt popped up behind her. "Why'd you come in so hot?"

"I'm nervous, okay? I have a man in my backseat with a gun pointed at me."

"Get out, slow and easy."

She opened the car door and planted one booted foot on the gravel. Gantt was beside her in a second, poking her in the ribs with the gun.

"You don't need that thing." She swiveled toward the trunk.

"Where are you going?"

"I have groceries back there." Her eyes widened as Liam appeared behind Gantt. Gantt's own eyes flicked when he noticed her expression, but already it was too late.

Liam had wrapped one arm around Gantt's neck, knocking his other against Gantt's wrist, dislodging his weapon with a sharp blow.

Katie dropped to the ground and grabbed the gun. She jumped to her feet, clutching the weapon in one trembling hand.

Gantt choked and clawed at Liam's forearm, pinned to his throat. "Let me go. All I want is answers."

"Nobody holds a gun on my woman." He kneed Gantt in the back, bringing him to his knees. "Katie, give me that gun before you shoot the wrong person."

She handed it over, glancing at Gantt doubled over in the dirt. "He didn't hurt me."

"Good, and now maybe I won't hurt him once he tells

me what the hell he's doing here." He waved the gun at Gantt. "Get up and head toward the cabin."

Gantt staggered to his feet, and Katie reached out to help him up.

Liam snapped. "Get away from him. Go ahead of us and unlock the door."

His tone brooked no disagreement. She jogged up the two steps to the cabin and unlocked the door, swinging it wide for Liam and his prisoner.

When they all got inside, Katie held up her finger. "I left the groceries and your clothes in the trunk."

"Leave it for now." He pointed the gun at one of the chairs in front of the fireplace. "Take a seat, Gantt, and start spilling."

Gantt collapsed in the chair, rubbing his throat. "You know all there is to know, McCabe. I busted out of the prison they called a training center."

"I need to know a lot more than that, Gantt, and I'm the one with the gun."

"You should know what happened better than anyone. Some pretty little nurse shot me up with a vitamin. Ha! If that was a vitamin, I'm the grand wizard of the Ku Klux Klan."

"It didn't affect you?"

"Oh, it affected me all right." He turned to Katie. "Ms. Locke, can I get some water?"

"You can call me Katie, and…"

Liam sliced his hand through the air. "He can wait a few minutes for the water."

"Liam…"

He shot her a look that cut to the bone. Maybe she wouldn't make a good spy, after all.

"How did it affect you, Gantt?"

"Knocked me out. Gave me weird dreams. When I came to, it took me a good fifteen minutes to remember who I was and what the hell I was doing in that place. Nobody else seemed bothered by it, and then you saw them at PT the next day—running like Usain Bolt and lifting weights like the Incredible Hulk. I'm no genius but I put two and two together."

Liam nodded. "Yeah, T-101 is no vitamin."

"T-101?"

Liam ignored him. "But it must've been something before that. You didn't plan your escape and that explosion in one day."

"I overheard a conversation between Hamilton and Moffitt. I had left my access card in my computer in the classroom. Mills wasn't there, but the door was ajar. Their voices were hushed, so of course I listened."

Katie held her breath as Liam asked, "What did you hear?"

"Crazy stuff. They were discussing our class of recruits and how they thought they'd respond to training and hold up in the field." He cleared his throat. "Normal stuff until they started mentioning all the Tempest agents who'd gone off the rails. I know all about post-traumatic stress, but the things they were talking about?" He shook his head. "Crazy stuff."

"You started planning your escape then?" Liam had relaxed his grip on the gun, but he still looked ready to pounce.

"I did. The night I ran into you at the parking garage, the plan was in its final stages." He hunched forward, his hands gripping his knees. "I almost confided in you that night. I knew you were different from the others."

"How?" Liam narrowed his eyes.

"First of all, if that fool Hamilton couldn't tell you'd already had some training or experience, he should lose his job."

"I was a SEAL. He probably put it down to that."

"I know, but there was something else about you. And then I could tell the vitamin shot hadn't affected you, either. You could still almost just keep up with the other guys, who were all pumped up on that stuff. T-101. But not quite."

"So, why didn't you? Confide in me?"

Gantt leaned back in the chair and winced. "It was that night at the parking garage when Ms. Locke, Katie, showed up."

Katie folded her arms. She knew it had been her fault. "Why did that stop you?"

He waved his finger between her and Liam. "You two obviously knew each other, and that made me have doubts about McCabe. I'd heard rumors about your...connection with Mr. Romo and that piece of work Ginger Spann. I thought it might be a setup. It might still be a setup."

Liam plucked at the rumpled guard shirt he was still wearing. "Yeah, I'm actually a security guard for Tempest."

"They know you're missing?"

"They do now."

Gantt chuckled. "Serves 'em right."

The tension seeped out of Katie's shoulders. The men seemed to be done circling and sniffing each other. "Can I get Dustin that water now?"

"Sure, if he promises not to toss it in my face."

"Man, I'm going to be too busy drinking it. That choke-hold you executed did a number on my throat."

"Like I said—" Liam winked "—nobody holds a gun to my woman."

Katie filled a glass with water from the tap and handed it to Gantt. "How have you been surviving out here?"

"Easy." He took the glass from her hand and downed half of it. "I'm a survivalist."

"How'd a survivalist end up taking a job with the government?" Liam shoved Gantt's weapon in the back of his waistband.

"Tempest never presented itself like that to me. I mean, I knew it was a government agency, but they emphasized that they flew under the radar. I guess I didn't realize how far under the radar a government agency could fly."

"You'd be surprised."

Gantt swirled the remaining water in his glass. "Are you going to tell me your story, McCabe?"

"Someday."

"That day had better be sooner rather than later if you expect my help taking down that facility."

Liam's expression never changed except for a flicker in his eye. "What makes you think that's our plan?"

"You wouldn't still be here if it wasn't." He jerked his chin toward the window. "You have a car, cash. If I'd had those things I'd be at the Mexican border by now."

"You're good, Gantt. Too good for Tempest."

Katie stuck her hand up in the air and waved. "Can I get those groceries now? I'm starving."

Gantt rose from his chair, but Katie held up her hand, palm forward. "Both of you guys are in hiding. I can handle the groceries."

She made two trips to bring in the groceries and Liam's clothes. She parked the bags on the counter and started pulling out the food. "I have bacon if one of you wants to cook it. I'll whip up some scrambled eggs and someone can oversee the toaster."

Liam raised his hand. "I think I'm qualified to watch the toaster."

"I can do the bacon." Gantt joined her in the kitchen and began banging the cupboard doors, looking for a skillet.

She shoved the toaster toward Liam and dropped a loaf of wheat bread next to it. "See to the toast, toast boy."

Liam untwisted the tie on the package. "Gantt, where were you staying all this time?"

He jerked his thumb at the side door. "In the woods."

While Gantt told Liam what he'd taken from Tempest and how he'd used it, Katie made the scrambled eggs and cooked some potatoes in the microwave. She diced the potatoes and cooked them in the leftover bacon grease.

She piled two plates with eggs, potatoes and bacon. "How's the toast coming along?"

"Four slices done and buttered."

She set the plates on the table for Liam and Dustin and then scooped the rest of the eggs onto a plate for herself.

They all sat down at the kitchen table, and Dustin pointed to her plate. "That's all you're having?"

She opened her mouth and Liam cut in. "She's a vegetarian."

Dustin broke off a piece of bacon and waved it at her. "You'd do okay in the woods. I could show you a lot of edible plants and berries, but you gotta watch some of those berries—poisonous."

"Thanks, I'll keep that in mind the next time I'm stranded in the woods."

"You keep hanging out with this guy—" he pointed his fork at Liam "—and that might be sooner than you think."

"Nope. She's getting out of here."

Katie rolled her eyes. "I'm not leaving, Liam. Now that we have Dustin here, we have a better chance than ever of stopping Tempest in its tracks."

"I'm in." Dustin stabbed a piece of egg, his jaw tight.

She grabbed Liam's wrist. "I haven't even told you my plan yet. I have unlimited access to Tempest's computer system now. Do you know what that means? Do you know how much power that gives me?"

"But Gantt and I can't even be there with you."

"You can be close. There are woods all around that facility." She leveled a finger at Dustin. "Who better to hang with in the woods than Mr. Survivalist himself?"

"Having you back in that nest of vipers with the head snake makes my stomach turn."

Gantt dropped his fork. "Mr. Romo? You got close to Mr. Romo? So the rumors were true?"

"Some of the rumors were true. He and Ginger invited me into their inner circle. They're trusting me with their computer system, but I'm not buddy-buddy with them."

Gantt gulped down some orange juice. "I heard it's not a buddy Mr. Romo wants. Or maybe it is, but it's a particular kind of buddy if you get my drift, and—" he glanced at Liam "—no offense."

"Oh, I can handle that part." She flicked her fingers, wishing Dustin hadn't reminded Liam of Mr. Romo's designs on her body. "That part of the initiation is off in the future. I'll be long gone by then—if Liam allows me to carry out this plan."

"Shoot." Liam pushed his plate away. "Let us in on this big plan."

She took a big breath and gripped the edge of the table. "I'm going to infiltrate the facility's main computer system and shut down everything—electricity, network, phones. You're going to tell all the recruits what's really going on, and once we have everyone out of there, we're going to do what you'd planned to do all along, Liam. We're going to blow the place sky high—literally."

Chapter Seventeen

Liam just about choked on his eggs. "You can do all that from a computer?"

"Pretty much, but I'm going to need your help with the recruits and the...uh...explosives."

Dustin got up from the table and gathered the plates. "I don't get it. If you have to be at Tempest to do all this stuff, where are you going to be? Once those systems start to shut down, aren't Romo and Spann to figure out it's you?"

"What he said." Liam stretched his legs in front of him. "And how do you blow up several buildings from a computer?"

"Like I said, I figured you two could come up with something for that." She brushed some crumbs from the table into her palm.

"What makes you think I'm hell-bent on destroying the Tempest facility? I'm here to gather intel." He shifted his gaze away from Gantt and his intent stare.

Katie folded her arms on the table and hunched forward. "Don't you think the intel you already gathered is sufficient cause to shut down the compound?"

"I think it's time that I checked in with—" he glanced at Gantt hanging on his every word "—checked in."

"I've been thinking about that, Liam. We're not too far

from Sun Valley. There have to be stores there with throw-away phones. I could head out there this afternoon and be back before dark."

"By yourself?" Every cell in his body protested. All this talk of blowing up Tempest and taking down computer systems gave him a strong desire to tuck Katie back into that bed and pull the covers over her head. Thankfully, she couldn't read his thoughts right now.

"Nobody is going to know me in Sun Valley. I doubt Tempest has spies covering the entire state of Idaho. I'm coming with you. I even have a disguise."

Gantt ducked his head. "I'm going to sit this one out. I need to get back to my camp in the woods. I have a cache of weapons buried out there. I'll work out a way for us to get close to Tempest, and once Katie shuts down the computer system, we can take care of the rest."

Crossing his arms, Liam studied Gantt's face. He had to trust the man at some point. He couldn't haul a captive around with him everywhere.

Katie spread her hands. "We'll meet back here for dinner?"

"This ain't no house party, Katie." Liam pushed back from the table and drained the rest of his orange juice.

"I realize that, and just to bring us all back to reality, who gets the gun?"

Gantt lifted a shoulder. "You can take it... I have others."

"You *are* good, Gantt. Did you take more than guns?"

"How the hell else are we gonna blow that place to smithereens?"

LIAM REFUSED TO stuff his body on the floor of the back-seat again, but he slumped down in the passenger seat, pulling the baseball cap over his eyes, until they cleared Elk Crossing.

The temperatures dropped even more, but the snow was a no-show even at the higher elevations.

Katie turned the heat on higher. "We might get lucky and find a phone in a convenience store on the way to Sun Valley and spare ourselves the drive."

"I don't mind the drive, and maybe I'll find some decent jeans over there." He poked himself in the thigh.

"You don't like the ones I picked out for you?"

"Is there such a thing as dad jeans? If so, I think I'm wearing them."

"Please, you look sexy in anything."

"I was thinking the same thing about you in those slacks and blouses buttoned up to your chin. No wonder Romo had singled you out." He reached over and tucked her wild hair behind her ear. "What did you think of Gantt?"

"I believe him. I trust him. Do you?"

"His story rings true, but I'm not sure he'll be at the cabin when we return."

"You're naturally suspicious. He'll be there. He really wants revenge on Tempest, don't you think?"

"Yeah, but he's a survivalist, and survivalists usually work alone. That's what surprises me about his employment with Tempest. His type usually doesn't trust the government."

"Maybe he got sick of living on roots and bark."

Liam drummed his fingers against the console. "Just makes me wonder what line Tempest fed him during the recruitment phase. They could've been more upfront about their objectives with someone like Gantt."

"Do you really think Gantt would go for...whatever it is Tempest is trying to accomplish with these assassinations?"

"I'm not sure, Katie." He skimmed his knuckles along her thigh, the denim of her jeans soft and worn. "Until I get the list of executions to Prospero, we have no idea what connects the victims. Some of these killings have been off the radar, set up as accidents."

"Will your agency be able to figure it all out?"

"We have some amazing analysts on board. I'm sure they'll see a pattern." He punched at the radio buttons. "Alternative rock?"

"Out here?" She snorted. "I doubt it. Go for the country. I can live with it—I did before."

"Before..." He traced the edge of her ear. "I never said I was sorry for leaving."

"Yes, you did. You said it a million times before you left."

"Before...they were just words before I left. Words I said to make you feel better, to make myself feel better." He smoothed his fingertip along the hard line of her jaw. "I never said sorry after, when I really meant it."

Her long lashes swept over her eyes. "You freed that doctor, didn't you? When I heard about it on the news, I knew it was you, your team. That doctor risked his life to help us, and then you risked your life to save him."

He stared past her out the window, recalling the doctor as they'd found him—filthy, gaunt, signs of torture on his body. That doctor had helped them, and they had to rescue him.

"Oh, I realize you can't acknowledge it, but I know it was your team, and for a little while I felt better about your abandonment."

His gaze shifted back to her face. "Only a little while?"

"Only when I wasn't missing you so much it hurt." She sniffed.

"I would've come back to you, Katie."

"I couldn't trust you anymore, Liam. You'd left me just like all the rest, just like all those families who'd promised to be my forever."

"Biggest mistake of my life. I want a do-over."

"I can't get punched in the gut again."

"Is that a no?"

"Our first convenience store." She veered off the highway and wheeled into the parking lot, dodging his question like a pro. "Maybe they sell phones here."

They walked into the store. Liam nodded at the clerk. "Do you sell prepaid, disposable phones?"

"We sure do, but I gotta warn you. The cell reception is bad here. You probably have to head into Sun Valley to get some decent air."

"That's where we were headed, anyway." He strolled to the aisle the clerk indicated while Katie stood before the refrigerators. "Do you want something to drink?"

"Soda." He pulled one of the phones from the rack and read the instructions. He had no idea if Prospero would even pick up from an unknown number, even if he did have all the right codes.

He met Katie at the register, and she pulled out her wad of cash to pay. He owed this woman more than money when all this was over, but she didn't seem to want anything more from him—probably wouldn't even take the money.

She put her drink in the cup holder and started the engine. "Do you want to continue to Sun Valley and have lunch? Pretend we have a normal life for an hour or two?"

"Sure. Gantt's not expecting us until later, anyway—if he shows up at all."

She hit the road and turned down the radio. "How did you end up with Prospero after leaving the navy? Or can't you tell me that?"

"I can tell you anything, Katie-O. You've earned it." He popped the tab on his can of soda and took a fizzy sip. "Prospero recruited me at the end of that last mission. I went through a training academy, similar to Tempest's but worlds apart in goals, objectives and methods."

"You mean they didn't drug you?"

"And no creepy leader. The man who heads up Prospero is admirable, a role model, one of the good guys."

"Your last mission was just two years ago. You haven't been with Prospero long, have you?"

"This is my first mission." He took another swig of soda to wash away the taste of failure in his mouth. "I was chosen because I'm new, young, unknown. Maybe they should've gone with a more experienced agent."

"You haven't failed, Liam, and you're not going to. Even Prospero must've realized there was a chance the T-101 would affect you. They must've warned you that you could become a Tempest agent for real. They knew the risks, and you were willing to take those risks for your agency."

The turn-off for the resort appeared, and Katie maneuvered the car onto the road that led to the main resort area.

Liam pointed to a few of the mountainsides with white dusting. "Looks like they're going the man-made route for some of the runs."

"Good, then we should be able to get lost in the crowd."

They rolled into the town and agreed on a restaurant that served just about everything. Once the hostess seated them in a corner booth, Liam pulled out the phone.

"I'm going to give this a try. I have Prospero's phone number memorized along with the access codes I need to get through."

The waitress hovered at their table and he ordered another soda while Katie requested some hot tea. When the waitress left, he punched in the Prospero number. He listened to a series of beeps and responded with the appropriate code. He went through this process two more times before he reached a ringing phone on the other end of the line.

He released a pent-up breath when he heard the clipped British tones of an analyst he knew. "Agent ID, please?"

Liam cupped his hand around the phone and recited his agent ID.

"This is Analyst Sharpe. How can I help you Agent McCabe?"

"Xander, you can cut the formal stuff. I need help."

"You're supposed to be in the Tempest training camp out in Idaho. What happened?"

"It was the T-101. They gave me a super dose of the stuff and I freaked out—lost my memory, escaped from the facility."

"You obviously recovered your memory. Did you get any intel before you abandoned ship?"

A muscle ticked in Liam's jaw. "I didn't abandon ship. I temporarily lost my mind and yes, I got some names and dates of assassinations, some that were staged as accidents, so maybe those were off our radar."

"Good job, Agent McCabe." Xander paused. "Can you relate that information to me now?"

"I have GPS coordinates and dates. Are you ready?"

"Fire away."

"And Xander?"

"Still here."

"The last set of coordinates is the White House."

"Got it. Ready to receive."

Katie waved the waitress away as Liam closed his eyes and retrieved the numbers from Patterson's notebook.

"That's it." A light sheen of sweat had broken out on his forehead, and he blotted it with a napkin.

"One more thing, Liam. Coburn's going to want to talk to you. Can he call you on the phone you're using?"

"Yes."

"He'll get back to you within the hour. Stay put."

He shoved the phone to the side of the table and gestured to the waitress. "The boss is going to call me back."

"That's good, right?"

He nodded and ordered a bowl of chili and some corn-bread from the waitress. Katie opted for some lentil soup and more hot water for her tea.

When the chili arrived he plunged his spoon into the steaming bowl. "What have you been up to the past few years? I know you're still in San Diego, and I know you're still designing video games. Have you been…dating?"

"Here and there. You?"

He stuffed down the jealousy. "Not much time for that with my schedule."

"I should tell you, though, I'm in love."

Her words slammed against his chest, and his hands curled into fists. Was this some kind of joke? After the way they'd made love last night, she'd made him feel like the only one—just as she was for him.

She smirked and pulled out her phone. "You deserved that, and I can't help myself. I'm a cruel witch."

She held out her phone to him. "I'm in love with this guy."

He'd never been so happy in his life to see a picture of a chocolate lab puppy, grinning from one floppy ear to the next.

"You got a dog."

"His name is Mario. A neighbor found a litter of abandoned puppies and of course, I had to take one in—one abandoned puppy to another."

He took the phone from her and traced his finger around Mario's head. "He looks like a handful."

"He is."

"Who's taking care of him?"

"The same neighbor who found him and kept his sister for herself. So he's having a holiday with his sister."

"But you miss him." He touched the corner of her turned-down mouth.

"Of course."

The phone on the table buzzed between them, bringing him back to his reality. He answered the phone with a code word, and Jack Coburn responded with the corresponding code word.

"You okay, McCabe? No residual effects from the T-101?"

"No, sir. None that I can detect."

"We'll get you a full medical when you get back. Good work on the coordinates. I think you just prevented an attack on the White House, son."

"I think so, too, sir. I'm sorry that I compromised the rest of the mission."

"How so? You didn't compromise anything."

"I let my feelings of disorientation get the best of me, and I escaped from the facility."

"I don't see that as a problem, McCabe. Where are you now? How are you surviving without money, a car? We don't even have any safe houses out that way."

Liam's gaze tracked to Katie, pouring herself another cup of tea. "I have some help on the outside, sir."

Coburn sucked in a breath. "Can you trust him?"

"With my life." He winked at Katie as she looked up. "Will we try to infiltrate another way?"

"Hell, no. We've still got you."

He glanced at Katie and shrugged. "What do you mean?"

"They double-dosed you with T-101 and you flipped out. In their eyes, the fact that the drug had its desired effect and you were able to escape is all good."

"I'm not sure I follow, sir."

"You're going back in, McCabe."

"Sir?"

"You go back to the Tempest facility with your tail between your legs, apologize for running off half-cocked and now you're more committed than ever to fulfilling your duties as a Tempest agent. They might still suspect you, but the fact that you returned is going to speak volumes to them."

He tried to ignore Katie's wide eyes. She couldn't hear Coburn's words, but his face must be betraying all kinds of emotions.

And the last one she'd see was satisfaction. Coburn was giving him the opportunity to redeem himself and the operation, to snatch victory from the jaws of defeat. And more important, he wouldn't have to send Katie back there on her own.

"Sounds like an excellent plan, sir. I'm on it."

"Now that we have further proof of Tempest's plans, you know the endgame, don't you, McCabe?"

"Alert the recruits and destroy the Tempest facility." Just as Katie had guessed.

Coburn ended the call with his assurances that any effects of the T-101 would be countered once he returned to the fold—if he returned to the fold.

"You look…happy. Is your boss giving you a bonus or something? Since I'm the one who got the notebook at great peril to my health and well-being, are you going to share that bonus?"

"I got a bonus, all right. I get to return to Tempest." He popped the last piece of cornbread into his mouth.

Katie's own mouth dropped open. "What does that mean? How can you possibly return to Tempest?"

"I do it as a contrite recruit who overreacted to the vitamin shot."

"You're willing to go back and poke the bear?"

He grabbed her hand. "I'll feel a lot better about having you go back there if I'm there with you."

"If they let you live." She reached out and twisted the front of his shirt in her fist. "I don't like it. They might continue to dose you with T-101 and then restrain you. What happens then?"

"It's my job, Katie. I'll figure it out."

"I'm scared." She covered her hands with her face. "I can't lose you, Liam, not again."

"Then we'd better make sure our plan works. Now get me and Gantt back to your place, so that he can set up in the woods and I can wander back to the facility on my own on Sunday."

They paid up and got back on the highway to Elk Crossing. When they arrived at the empty cabin, Liam placed the gun and his phone on the kitchen counter next to a piece of paper.

He picked up the paper and turned it toward Katie. "It's a map of the woods. Looks like Gantt's campground."

"And you thought he wouldn't be here."

"He's not here."

"It's not six o'clock yet, and he left us directions to his campsite. Do you think he wants us to go get him?"

"We're not doing that. We're not walking into a possible trap."

"I think the guy is trustworthy."

"We'll see."

They waited for over an hour, during which time Katie cooked some pasta and had him chopping tomato, basil and garlic.

He pulled his phone toward him. "After six, no Gantt."

As she stirred the pasta in the boiling water, Katie bit her bottom lip. "You don't think he's planning to double-cross us, do you?"

"What happened to trusting the guy? He's ten minutes late, and now he's in league with the devil?"

"Well, what do you think?"

"I think he probably thought better of joining a team,

since it worked out so well for him last time. The guy's a loner and he'll stay a loner."

"He still may show up."

The time ticked on and still no Gantt. They ate the pasta and some salad and saved the leftovers for Gantt.

"We're going to have to leave without him tomorrow morning, Katie. I need to get back to Tempest and turn myself in."

Her nose wrinkled as she washed up the last of the dishes. "I just don't get it. He was so gung-ho to take his revenge on Tempest."

"The guy is an enigma. I don't know what happened, but I'm going to keep that gun under my pillow tonight."

He built up the fire again and they sat before it, filling each other in on the details of their lives in the past two years. He didn't know how he was going to convince her to take him back, but he was determined to be a part of her life again.

And he knew one method of persuasion that she couldn't resist. He took her face, warmed by the fire, in his two hands and kissed her mouth thoroughly. "Let's go to bed."

After they'd made love, he tucked her against his side and put the gun within reach on the nightstand. If Gantt or anyone else was lurking outside and decided to break into the cabin in the dead of night, he'd get a nasty surprise.

But the night passed without incident, and Katie cooked up the last of the eggs the next morning.

He hunched over the counter, Gantt's map between his hands. He flicked his finger at an X with a circle around it.

"I wonder what this is."

Katie leaned over his shoulder, holding a plate of steaming food. "Looks important."

Liam snapped his fingers. "Gantt said he'd taken several weapons from Tempest and buried his cache. I wonder if they're here. Maybe he left them for us, and they'd definitely come in handy."

"So, we *are* going to his campsite before we go back?"

"I think it's worth the risk."

"Just like you think returning to Tempest is worth the risk. Seems like you think a lot of things are worth risking your life over."

"A lot of things for me, but not you. You're not going to risk your life, so you drive me to the edge of these woods down the road and wait. I'll see if I can find his cache of weapons. If not, I'll be back at the car as soon as I can. If anything else happens, you leave me."

"Yeah, right."

"I mean it, Katie."

"Gotcha."

He tugged on a lock of her hair. Stubborn woman wouldn't do a thing he told her to do.

They cleaned up the cabin and Liam changed back into the security guard uniform. Rolling up the sleeves, he said, "That's one thing I'm looking forward to back at Tempest—my own clothes."

"If they let you live long enough to change into them." Katie dropped her purse at the front door and rushed into his arms. "I don't want you to go back there."

He crushed her to his chest and stroked her wavy hair. "I don't want you to go back there, either."

She murmured into his shoulder. "It's different for me. I didn't escape. I'm not under suspicion."

"You don't know that. Don't get too complacent, Katie. Be careful."

"I will, and I'm not giving them much time to get suspicious. As soon as I'm able and you're ready, we're shutting it down."

They packed up the car, and Katie checked out.

When she got back behind the wheel, Liam asked from

the backseat, "Did the manager mention anything about Dustin?"

"Didn't say a word about him or you. Asked if I'd enjoyed my stay and despite everything, after the two nights we shared, I couldn't wipe the smile off my face when I told him I'd had the best two days of my life."

"He must've figured you'd led a boring life up to this point."

"I wish." She pulled away from the cabins and when she'd made the turn to the main road, he climbed into the front seat and smoothed Gantt's map on his knee. "Just a half a mile to the next turnout on your right."

"Is his campsite far from the road?"

"Maybe a quarter of a mile in. Shouldn't take me more than ten minutes in and ten minutes out, depending on the terrain. Give me another ten minutes to dig where X marks the spot, so I'm talking forty minutes tops. I'm not back here in forty minutes, you take off."

She didn't respond, even after he stared at her profile for several seconds. He heaved out a breath and tucked the map into his pocket. He then checked the chamber of the gun and held it loosely in his lap. He had to prepare for an ambush, but if Gantt had buried a stash of weapons, he wanted to get his hands on them.

Katie pointed ahead. "There's the turnoff."

When she parked, he turned to her and kissed her hard. "I'll be back in forty."

"I'll be here."

He slipped from the car pushing the door closed and then crept into the woods, Gantt's map burned into his brain. They'd done some tracking and survivalist training at the Prospero academy, so he had a handle on this.

He noticed some freshly broken twigs and dirt covering newly fallen leaves, indicating that someone had come this way recently. Gantt had planned to return to his site when he and Katie had left for Sun Valley. Maybe he should've insisted that Gantt come with them just to keep an eye on him.

Several feet from the campsite, Liam circled around from the other side, bordered by a dense thicket of trees. He crept forward, watching the ground to avoid dry leaves and twigs.

As he drew abreast of the campsite, he looked up, searching for a break in the trees and a clear view of the space.

He crouched forward, peering through a gap in the branches.

He'd just found Dustin Gantt—tied to a tree, his throat slit.

Chapter Eighteen

Katie hummed to the country song on the radio and glanced at the clock on the dashboard. Fifteen minutes and counting. As if she'd leave Liam in there after forty minutes or forty hours. She'd never leave him.

The tap at the window sent her straight to the roof of the car. She jerked her head to the side, and the relief coursing through her body almost made her weak. She hadn't realized how tense she'd been since Liam had loped off into the forest.

She unlocked the door and he burst into the car, his breathing heavy, his face flushed.

"What's wrong?"

"Hit it! Hit the gas."

She cranked on the engine and peeled away from the turnout, her back tires fishtailing and spewing gravel and dirt in their wake.

She didn't say another word until they made it to the highway. Gripping the steering wheel, she finally asked, "What happened back there?"

"Someone killed Dustin Gantt."

She gasped and tightened her hold on the steering wheel. "You saw him."

"Someone had slit his throat."

The blood pounded in her temples, and she panted for air.

"I'm sorry," Liam said as he rubbed her thigh.

"Did you see anything else?" Her voice seemed unnaturally high and disembodied to her own ears.

"I didn't stick around to see anything else. Believe me, I wanted to dig up that cache of weapons, but I thought someone might still be watching the area. I couldn't even be sure they didn't have a drone in the area. All I could think of was getting back to you and getting you out of there."

"How did they find him?"

"Not sure. The tracker was tracked."

"Oh, my God." She placed a hand over her thumping heart. "What if they had tracked him when he was at the cabin with us?"

"If they had, they would've stuck around and waited for us."

"Do you think Dustin told them anything about us?"

He didn't answer her, and she slid a glance at his white face and hard jaw.

After several seconds he passed a hand across his face. "Dustin Gantt didn't give them anything—guaranteed."

She was afraid to ask more, so she drove on. "Nothing changes, Katie. Drop me off somewhere before you get to your place, and I'll make my way back to Tempest this afternoon. You go back into work as usual Monday morning. Got it?"

"I do. And don't worry about those weapons." Tears stung her nose. "I'll get you access to whatever you want. Dustin showed us the way, and now they have even more to answer for."

The trip passed too quickly and all too soon, Liam was directing her off the road.

He turned to her and grabbed her by the shoulders. "Whatever happens in the next forty-eight hours, just know that I love you, Katie-O."

He slammed the car door before she could respond, so she whispered it to his back as she watched him through the window. "I love you, too, Liam McCabe."

SHE SMOOTHED HER hand along the front of her pleated, gray slacks and pressed the button of the elevator in the parking garage. Stepping inside, she pushed the button for her level with her knuckle.

She hadn't seen any ambulances, fire trucks or armed guard this morning, so whatever they'd done to Liam, they'd done it privately and under cover of Tempest security.

Her gut knotted as she got off on her floor and forced her feet to move one in front of the other to her office.

Her ears tuned in to the idle chatter from the help desk bullpen and the other cubicles, but the only discussion of murder and mayhem she heard came from people recapping their weekend TV viewing.

She sat in front of her computer and logged in. Two instant messages popped up. One came from Liam:

I'm in.

She closed her eyes and took two deep breaths.
The second one was from Ginger:

Urgent, call when you get in.

The tension seized her muscles once again. Ginger and Mr. Romo must want to discuss these latest developments with her.

Since Liam's message had come in earlier, she didn't dare answer him now. Instead, she responded to Ginger that she was in the office and ready to meet.

She jumped at the alacrity of Ginger's response:

Elevator now.

Her fingers itched at the work to be done on the computer system, but she wanted the details on the return of the Prodigal Son, so she snatched her access card from her computer's card reader and headed out to the executive elevator.

In a first, Ginger beat her to it and greeted her with a grim smile and a bland question. "Did you have a nice weekend?"

"I did, thanks. You?"

"No."

The elevator doors opened, and Ginger ushered her in first. They rode in silence.

As soon as the doors opened on Mr. Romo's floor, Ginger blew out a noisy breath. "McCabe returned."

"What?" Katie tripped to a stop in front of Mr. Romo's office door. "Why did he do that?"

Ginger nudged her into the office with a little push. "Sit."

She greeted Mr. Romo and sat in her customary chair across from him as he balanced his laptop on his knees. What did he do on that thing all day?

Folding her arms across her chest, she asked, "When did McCabe return?"

"Yesterday, late afternoon, disheveled, a little worse for wear, but contrite." Mr. Romo snapped his laptop shut.

"Where had he been?" Katie scooted to the edge of her chair, arms still crossed.

Ginger wedged one slim hip against the arm of the couch, next to Mr. Romo. "Wandering around the woods, apparently, still wearing the guard uniform he'd stolen off Meyers's back."

"Did he tell you why he escaped?"

Mr. Romo stroked his beard with two fingers. "He had a bad reaction to our vitamin formula, went a little crazy."

Katie narrowed her eyes. "Do you believe him?"

"Maybe." Mr. Romo exchanged a look with Ginger that made her believe one of them wasn't buying it.

"Do you think the same thing could've happened to Dustin Gantt? The vitamin hit him the wrong way and he lost it?"

Ginger's eyes flickered at Gantt's name. "But you told us there were indications in his browsing history that he'd been planning some kind of escape."

"That's true." She'd really just wanted to mention Gantt's name in their presence to gauge their reactions, and Ginger hadn't disappointed.

"And you said McCabe had no such indications." Mr. Romo drummed his fingers on top of his laptop. "That's still the case, isn't it, Katie? You didn't discover anything more about McCabe over the weekend, did you? No connection to Gantt?"

She'd discovered all kinds of delicious things about Liam over the weekend, but she'd be damned if she'd share any of it with them. "Nothing and no association with Gantt, but I did discover additional info about Gantt. He'd been doing some research on survivalist websites. What do you think that means?"

Mr. Romo flicked his fingers in the air. "We don't care about Gantt. What's done is done. If he attempts to reveal any top secret information he learned here, we'll go through the appropriate authorities."

They obviously hadn't gone through any appropriate authorities to murder him, which was why Gantt's disappearance was suddenly off the table, a nonissue.

"What's going to happen to McCabe? A-are you going to fire him or whatever you call it?"

Mr. Romo spoke up, a little too loudly. "He's too valuable to discharge—a prime specimen, former navy SEAL, and now apparently loyal as hell."

"We don't know if that's the real reason he returned." Ginger rested a hand on Mr. Romo's shoulder. "It could be some sort of ploy."

Mr. Romo's cold eyes grew icier as he rolled his shoulder, shrugging off Ginger's hand.

Ginger snorted in a quick breath, her nostrils flaring.

Someone would pay for her dissension in front of the new girl.

"How can I help?" Katie folded her hands in her lap, all eager schoolgirl. "What do you want me to do?"

"Watch him through his computer activity as you'd planned to do. He rested last night and is ready to resume his regular schedule today, including classroom instruction." Mr. Romo smiled, and the ice in his eyes cracked just a little. "Report anything suspicious back to us, of course."

"Of course." She twisted her fingers into knots. "Are you going to try a different vitamin formula on him?"

"Perhaps."

Ginger rose from the couch and stepped between her and Mr. Romo. "That's not your concern, KC."

Mr. Romo hunched forward and nudged Ginger's hip to get her to move to the side. "She's just trying to be helpful, Ginger."

Ginger's eyes blazed for a moment before she eked out a tight smile. "Of course she is."

Ginger Spann was a liar. She'd claimed to harbor no jealousy over Mr. Romo's interest in her, but there it was—in her eyes. And it could mean trouble.

Hopefully, Katie would be long gone before Ginger could unleash the green-eyed monster.

Katie hopped up from the chair. "I'll get right to work tracking McCabe and anyone else you need to look at."

"You're a good little soldier, KC." Ginger took her arm

and began maneuvering her out of the office. If this was to avoid Mr. Romo's creepy group grope-hug, she was all for it.

"KC," Mr. Romo called from his position on the couch, and Ginger had to stop hustling her out of the room, even though her fingers still dug into Katie's arm.

"Yes?" *No hug, no hug, no hug.*

"We'll find a place for you in our new situation."

"New situation?" She shook off Ginger's hold.

"Because of all the problems we're having with the re-cruits here, we're speeding up their training. They'll be ready to roll in their new positions within the week."

"I hope you do—have a place for me. I feel like I've come home."

Ginger was back, placing her hand on Katie's back this time. "That's wonderful, now, first things first."

Ginger practically shoved her into the elevator, and then held the door open with one hand. "Tell me, KC. Did you ever run into someone named Sebastian Cole when you were being shunted from foster family to foster family in San Diego?"

Katie's heart slammed against her rib cage and she could barely breathe, but she furrowed her brow and tilted her head. "Sebastian Cole? No, I don't think so, but it's possible. Is he someone you know?"

"Yes, someone I knew."

"If you have a picture of him I might recognize him, but it's been almost ten years since I left the system."

"I don't have a picture, just wondering." She let her hand slide from the door, and the elevator closed with Ginger still staring at her.

She slumped against the side of the car. What was that all about? Had Ginger been doing more investigating? Katie hadn't wiped out her time in the foster care system in San Diego, but she'd cleansed any connection she and

Sebastian had in that system. There was no way Ginger could tie them together, but she had to watch her back. Ginger was on the warpath.

She dropped into the chair at her desk and logged in to her computer. With the recruits shipping out soon and Ginger giving her the once-over, she and Liam didn't have any time to lose. It was obvious that Mr. Romo accepted Liam's story, and Ginger had her doubts. As long as Katie could keep shoring up Liam's credentials, she could keep Ginger and Mr. Romo at bay.

Maybe she could shut down the facility as early as tonight. Would Liam be ready?

She couldn't wait to see him again. She'd have to devise some plan to go out to the recruit barracks.

A couple of keystrokes later and she'd brought down a few more of the recruits' laptops. She shot off a quick email to Ginger that she needed to investigate something on McCabe's laptop, and Ginger's okay came through in a flash—maybe too fast.

Katie gathered her notebook just to look official and made her way across the facility to the recruits' area.

She hovered at the doorway of the main classroom just as Mr. Mills was taking a seat behind his desk.

She tapped on the door and he looked up, unable to mask the scowl that had twisted his features. "You again?"

"Sorry. I was monitoring the laptops and noticed some irregularities. Somehow there are viruses that are sneaking through, and they're disrupting the automatic backups."

"Maybe Romo should worry less about computer viruses and more about the mental health of the recruits around here."

A chink in the armor? Katie wedged her shoulder on the doorjamb. "Are you talking about Dustin Gantt? I'd heard he hadn't been too stable when he walked through these doors to begin with."

"Is that what Mr. Romo tells you behind closed doors?" This time he didn't even attempt to keep the sneer out of his tone.

She shoved off the door and strolled into the classroom, and Mills's eyes popped at her approach, already regretting his words.

"I—I mean if Mr. Romo believes Gantt was on the edge, it must be true."

"If that's how you feel about Mr. Romo—" she sat on the edge of a desk "—why don't you leave Tempest?"

"I'm perfectly content here."

She shrugged and flipped her ponytail over her shoulder. "Doesn't sound like it. Is there someone other than Gantt having…difficulties?"

"Not that I know of."

"McCabe…"

Mills jumped from behind his desk. "I didn't say anything about McCabe."

Katie widened her eyes. "No, I did. His is one of the wonky laptops. Will he be coming to class soon?"

"They'll all be showing up in about ten minutes. Do you want to set up in the other classroom again?"

"That'll work. Can you send McCabe over first?"

"Why him?" Mills was gripping the edge of his desk.

She and Liam just might have an ally in Mr. Mills. He was looking out for Liam. He was worried about him, afraid she had some kind of torture in store for him for escaping.

"No reason. I need to see him and Kenneth Chang."

"I'll send McCabe over first with his laptop and Chang next."

"I appreciate that, Mr. Mills." She hopped off the desk and tucked the notebook under her arm. Turning when she reached the door, she said, "You really should think about leaving Tempest."

She went into the other classroom and paced the floor until Liam showed up. She almost ran across the room and jumped into his arms.

"Have a seat and log in to your computer, Mr. McCabe."

He let the door slam behind him. "Have I been a bad boy again, Ms. Locke?"

"The worst."

He sauntered toward her, placed the laptop on a desk between them and leaned forward. In a husky voice, he said, "I think I prefer you wearing decidedly fewer items of clothing."

Her gaze darted over his shoulder at the door. "Quiet."

"I thought that was quiet."

"Sit down, log in and tell me what happened."

He complied and started talking. "I staggered back through the gates yesterday afternoon. The guard at the gate freaked out, pulled a gun on me. I babbled on about losing my memory, losing my mind, and he called good old Dr. Nealy."

"Nealy? He's the head psychiatrist?"

"Yeah, a real mad-scientist type. I have no doubt in my mind he knows all about the effects of T-101. I'm not sure about the others."

"What did Nealy do?"

"Talked to me, deemed me sane enough to return to my room and then called Romo."

"Did you see Romo?"

"Apparently, he reserves that favor for you and Ginger."

She pinched his forearm. "Shut up."

"Did they tell you about me?"

"Yes. In a twist, I got the impression that Romo believed you, and Ginger did not."

"That's because she's tougher than he is. He hides away while she does all the dirty work."

"You might be right." She held her bottom lip between her teeth while she tapped some keys on his keyboard.

"What's wrong?" He scooted his chair closer.

"I think…" She twisted her ponytail around her hand.

"You think what?" He toyed with her fingers as they rested on the keyboard. "We're in this together, Katie-O. You can't keep things from me, not anymore."

"Like how I feel about you?"

He squeezed her fingers. "Like that."

"Is that why you left? Because I never told you I loved you?"

"I left because I was an immature idiot. I knew how you felt about me. Your actions couldn't have been clearer. That's all I should've needed. I still had to go on that last mission, but I should've insisted that you wait for me."

"And I should've told you I loved you, because I did and still do—with all my heart, and now we have to get out of here, Liam. The plan is to speed up your training and ship you out of here before any more of you go off the rails."

"I figured that. Is that what was worrying you before?"

She had to be able to trust him, to confide everything to him with no fear. "I think Ginger has it in for me now because she's jealous of Mr. Romo's…admiration for me."

"Admiration?" He raised his brows until they disappeared beneath the golden lock of hair curling over his forehead. "Is that what they're calling wanting to get in someone's pants these days?"

"That's what I'm calling it. She'd claimed she wasn't the jealous type, but she lied. She asked me about Sebastian today."

"How the hell did she put that together?"

"She hasn't put anything together—yet. I never scratched my background in the San Diego foster care system, and Sebastian shared that same background. Let's face it, that background is something that's very attractive to Tempest, isn't it?"

"That's for sure. She's just grasping at straws, but we don't want to waste any more time."

"Prospero isn't like that, is it? I mean, look at your family—the four of you boys, rambunctious, competitive, close, parents still married after thirty years, can't get more all-American than that."

Her tone must've sounded as wistful as she felt because Liam brushed a knuckle across her cheek. "And I took that family away from you when I left."

She shook her head. "They never belonged to me in the first place."

"Sure, they did." He grinned. "You should've heard the scolding I got from my mom for letting you go. She said even with the nose ring, you were the best thing that ever happened to me. And I didn't even tell her about the tattoo."

She sniffed and then Liam snatched his hand back when the door to the classroom opened. Chang looked inside. "Mills told me you need my laptop."

"I'll be calling you in about five minutes, okay?"

"Whatever."

She wrinkled her nose. "Full of charm, that guy, but you know what?"

"What?" He logged off his computer.

"I think we can use Mills."

"Mills can't stand you."

"Because he can't stand Mr. Romo and Ginger. He thinks I'm part of their axis of evil." She crossed one leg over the other and tucked her hands between her thighs so she wouldn't start pawing Liam. "He actually criticized Mr. Romo to me. Backtracked like hell after, but he'd already put it out there. He might be helpful when it comes time to get the rest of the recruits out of here."

"Tomorrow. Can we start tomorrow? With the information Gantt gave me and your magic tricks on the computer, I think we can shut this place down tomorrow night."

"I think so, too. I'm ready."

He chucked her beneath the chin. "Then why the sad face?"

"What happens to us after Tempest?"

"I have a brilliant idea, but I'll save it for later. Don't worry, Katie-O. I'm not leaving you again."

Chapter Nineteen

The following day Katie did bug fixes for Frank in between checking the computers for the major systems on the facility—electric, networks, telephones, security. She could shut them all down with a few clicks on her keyboard.

Liam planned to approach Mr. Mills today, perhaps even show him Garrett Patterson's notebook and the significance of his notations. Mills and Patterson had shared several interests and had lunched together on occasion. Maybe Patterson had even relayed some of his fears to Mills about the direction Tempest was taking.

And when it was all over? She couldn't wait to hear Liam's brilliant idea.

She'd reported to Mr. Romo that since tracking Liam's keystrokes, nothing had jumped out at her as being unusual. She'd protect that man with her last breath if that's what it took.

The hours dragged by, and a heavy air hung over the office. Clouds had been gathering all day, ominous dark clouds threatening the first snow of the season. But the atmosphere inside carried the same sense of breathless anticipation—or she was just projecting.

If any of the civilians had heard about another recruit's escape from the compound and subsequent return, they weren't talking about it. They weren't talking about much of anything. Could just be the midweek doldrums settling in.

She'd received two instant messages from Liam, one indicating that Mills was in and one giving her the green light for tonight.

The electricity would go first. In case facilities put some type of generator into play, she'd take down the network next—no computer access. She'd already been playing with jamming the cell tower and virtually putting a halt to all cell phone calls into and out of the facility. The security systems had been a piece of cake—all cameras would be disabled, all security doors deactivated.

She had plans to meet Liam outside the facility once she'd shut it down, and he'd have free rein to set up the explosive devices. She'd leave her car here, if necessary. Otherwise, she'd blow past the parking kiosk at the main gate, which would also be disabled.

She plucked her cell phone from her purse and brought up her photos. She tapped one of Sebastian, enlarging it, and traced over his face, his big smile. She whispered. "This is for you, brother."

The five o'clock hour crept up, and Frank stopped by her cubicle. "Are you working late again, KC?"

Stretching her arms over her head, she nodded. "Do you have anything else for me?"

"Nah, I got the word." He winked. "You're Mr. Romo's and Ginger's now."

She gulped, her hands dropping to her lap. "What does that mean? I still work for you, Frank."

"I know you're taking orders from them now, and that's okay. No worries. Hey, we all gotta climb that ladder somehow."

A flash of heat claimed her chest. "I'm not trying to

climb any ladder. I'm working on a special project for them."

He held up his hands. "Hey, whatever. No worries. I'm heading out of here. See you tomorrow?"

"I'll be here, same time, same place."

"Have a good one." He saluted.

Ugh, did everyone in the entire company think she was in some weird relationship with Ginger and Mr. Romo? Why hadn't Romo ever bothered to conceal his proclivities? And Ginger seemed proud of their affair. What self-respecting working woman would get confirmation out of sleeping her way to the top?

The sounds of the office packing up and leaving for the evening had her blood percolating. They planned to give everyone a chance to clear out, even Mr. Romo and Ginger.

Once the Prospero analysts put together those puzzle pieces from Garrett Patterson's notebook, and the CIA got some of the other Tempest employees to spill their guts, the gloves were off. The CIA would come down hard on Tempest and the likes of Mr. Romo and Ginger and all the doctors working on the T-101 formula.

There would be a formal investigation into Patterson's death and Samantha's and Dustin Gantt's, if they ever recovered his body.

All that had to happen and would happen, but Prospero couldn't wait for the formal investigation. Outside of anything sanctioned by the CIA or anything legal, for that matter, Tempest had to be stopped now—and Liam was the man to do it.

Katie had all the processes set up and ready to go. She'd kept the security cameras running so she could monitor everyone's departure.

How had Dustin put it? They didn't want to hurt anyone who didn't deserve it. For most of the people working at Tempest, it was just a high-paying government job that required secret and top secret clearance. They hadn't signed on for assassination and murder—Samantha hadn't.

She finished up the bug fixes Frank had given her just to occupy her time and her mind—the software programs they managed would never benefit from these fixes.

The sun had set, still obscured by the clouds, and the night got darker, the clouds more threatening.

She watched the last of the Tempest employees leave the building. She tracked the final cars on their passage from the parking structure.

Then she took a deep breath and put the first aspect of the plan into motion. She shut down the security cameras for everyone but her. Then she got to work on the access card system, virtually unlocking every door at the facility, making even high-security areas accessible to anyone. She'd already played with this system earlier in the day to give Liam access to the materials he needed.

She put the electrical system in jeopardy next, timing the shut-down of different areas, so security wouldn't be thrown into a panic.

Her fingers hovered over her keyboard. Next…

"Working late again?"

A chill dripped down Katie's spine as she looked up into the cool, green eyes of Ginger Spann.

"I usually do." She tapped the last key on her keyboard to complete the electrical shutdown, and still holding Ginger's gaze, she double-clicked on the program that would bring down the network.

"Stop clicking away on that keyboard, KC, and come with me."

"Come with you?" Luckily, Ginger was not computer savvy and wouldn't have the slightest clue what Katie had up on her screen, even if it wasn't turned away from Ginger's prying eyes. "I was just wrapping up, getting ready to leave for the night."

Ginger's eyes glittered with a strange light. "Oh, but tonight is the night."

Was she drugged up? Katie's heart did a double-time beat in her chest. *She knew.*

"The night for what? It's a Tuesday, no maintenance scheduled, no backups to monitor."

Ginger reached forward and stroked Katie's hair. "Get your mind off computers for a few minutes. Tonight's the night you're going to join Mr. Romo."

Dread thumped against the base of Katie's skull, but she still had work to do. She entered the shut-down code for the network and put it on a timer. Nothing was going into or out of this facility.

She finally logged off her computer and swiveled her chair around to face Ginger. "I don't understand. I thought I could go at my own pace with all that."

"Your pace is too slow. Mr. Romo has a comfortable area off his office. He and I spend a lot of time there, and now we want to share that time with you."

Could she pretend to go with her and then make a run for it at the elevator? She couldn't escape from her cubicle without doing physical harm to Ginger—not that the idea didn't appeal to her, but she didn't even have any weapons—except for the scissors in her desk drawer.

"I don't know, Ginger. I'm not ready." She plucked at her dark slacks and prim blouse. "I'm not dressed for it."

Ginger chuckled. "Don't worry about that. You won't be dressed for long."

Why tonight of all nights? It couldn't be a coincidence. Katie tucked her access card into her badge holder, left it on her desk and retrieved her purse from her desk drawer for the last time.

"I—I'm afraid I'm going to be such a disappointment to Mr. Romo. I'm not what he thinks I am."

"Maybe not. We'll see."

Hooking her purse over her shoulder, Katie pushed back from her chair. She followed Ginger, with her perfect posture, down the passageway between two rows of cubicles into the help desk bay.

Katie snapped her fingers. "Oh, wait. I left my access badge on my desk."

"Won't do you much good tonight."

"Oh?"

"For some reason, the door to this office didn't respond to my access badge. I walked right in."

"That's not right. Do you want me to look into that?" She'd taken several steps away from Ginger back to her cubicle. If she could stash those scissors in her purse, she might have a fighting chance.

Ginger placed a fingertip on her chin. "Can you really do something about the access badges, KC? I thought you were a computer programmer."

Katie's heart skipped a beat. She'd fallen into a trap. "Well, a lot of security systems are computerized, so it's the same thing."

"Imagine that."

Katie slipped around the corner into her cubicle, eased open her desk drawer, lifted the scissors and dropped them into her purse. She grabbed her badge holder and clutched it in her hand as she returned to Ginger, patiently waiting by the office door.

"You wouldn't want to forget your badge. How would you log in tomorrow morning and be able to do all of those amazing computer acrobatics that Mr. Romo loves so much?"

Katie managed a weak smile but her stomach churned with fear. Ginger had the look of a predator toying with her prey.

She lagged behind Ginger as they approached the executive elevator. Ginger stabbed at the button, but it remained dark, and the elevator didn't shift into action.

"Well, look at that. The access badges and now the elevator. What next?"

"This probably isn't a good night to get together. Facilities will be working all over the building if there are problems." She started backing away from Ginger. If she turned and ran now, Ginger might just think she was afraid of having sex with Mr. Romo. If she went along with Ginger, how would she get out of that office? Liam expected her to be off the grounds by now.

"Nonsense. Whatever facilities is up to, they know better than to disturb Mr. Romo. We'll take the stairs."

She took Katie's arm, but Katie spun away from her, clutching her purse to her chest, reaching inside for the scissors.

"You can't run from us, KC."

Katie heard the distinctive click of a gun safety, the same noise she'd heard from Dustin Gantt's gun as he hid in the backseat of her car a hundred years ago.

Katie turned slowly, brandishing the scissors in front of her. She stared down the barrel of the gun Ginger had pointed at her.

"Wh-what's going on?"

Ginger's jaw hardened. "Go ahead of me in the stairwell and keep your mouth shut."

Katie glanced outside before tugging open the door of the stairwell.

Where was Liam and what was he doing? If all went as planned, he'd be blowing up this building in less than twenty minutes—and now she was trapped inside.

Chapter Twenty

All of the lights went dead in the recruits' training area, but nobody cared. Half of the recruits were ready to bolt, half had jobs to do and the remaining staff had been restrained or were oblivious to the mutiny around them.

Gantt's escape and Liam's breakdown had already planted seeds of mistrust in most of the recruits' minds. Mills had been an easy convert, just as Katie had predicted. He'd been friends with Garrett Patterson, and Patterson had been hinting at Tempest's dark deeds.

The recruits trusted Mills, trusted what he had to say. Mills was ready to lead the majority of them out of here as soon as the fireworks started to distract security and the parking attendant at the kiosk. Liam warned the recruits that the CIA would most likely be conducting interviews with them once they were out of here and since they'd done nothing wrong, it was in their best interests to come clean about all their suspicions regarding the activities at Tempest.

Now Liam and a few diehards—Charlie, Tammy and surprisingly, Chung—were ready to set the explosions that would allow the rest to go free.

He eyed the helicopter on the top of Katie's building. Romo and Ginger would most likely escape unless he could get a jump on them, but he was willing to let them go and catch up with them later to get all the recruits out of here safely.

He even had a speech prepared over the loudspeaker to warn them of the coming disaster. Not that Romo and Ginger didn't deserve to die for what they'd done to so many people, but he was no judge, jury and executioner. He'd let the CIA handle those two, unless by some miracle he could capture them first.

"Are we ready?" Charlie's shaved head gleamed in the darkness.

Tammy responded. "When the explosions go off here and the remaining psychologists stagger outside, we round them up, right?"

"Right. I'll count down from ten and then it's go time."

Their breaths huffed out in the night air as Liam barked out the countdown. "Three, two, one, go!"

They each ran off to their positions, and a series of explosions rocked the ground. Smoke, shouts, screams and confusion swirled around him—chaos, just what they needed.

Before he reached the office building he glanced behind him in time to see the gates go down and the parking kiosk go sky-high.

He crept around the perimeter of the building and planted the explosive devices in the spots designed to do the most structural damage to the building. Maybe he could force Romo and Ginger out of the building before they had time to prepare the helicopter.

Katie was supposed to be monitoring the parking garage to make sure all the cars got out, but he decided to do a quick reconnaissance of the structure. His gaze swept the empty bottom level, and then he jogged up to the second level. His heart stopped before his feet did.

Katie's little car still huddled in its familiar spot. Had she left it here? Gone out on foot?

When would she have had time to do that? She couldn't still be here. She'd shut down all the systems, just as she'd promised.

Uneasiness caused a cold sheen of sweat to break out over his body, and he pulled the weapon from his waistband, the gun made possible by Katie's manipulation of the security access system. The woman was a genius.

He was going up to get Romo and Ginger. If they wouldn't come out, he had the exploding building as a backup. If they made their escape in the helicopter, the CIA could take care of them later.

He crept past the executive elevator and entered the stairwell. He took the first flight of stairs two at a time and then almost tripped over a shoe on the next landing.

He crouched down and swept it up in one hand. Black, round toe, sensible heel—exactly the type of shoe Katie O'Keefe would laugh at, but exactly the type KC Locke had been wearing in her undercover role as computer geek.

KATIE COVERED HER ears at the next explosion. Everything was going as planned—except this. She glanced at Romo and Ginger in the corner, heads together, whispering.

"The explosions are getting closer, you know, headed this way."

Mr. Romo clicked his tongue. "KC, KC. McCabe isn't going to blow up this building with you in it, is he?"

"I guess the laugh's on you because I'm not supposed to be here. He doesn't know I'm in here."

"It's too bad, you know. We really did trust you. We wanted you to be one of us—until one of our loyal employees spotted you in Elk Crossing."

"The same employee that killed Dustin Gantt?"

"No, actually, a different one—your hapless boss, Frank Norton. He tattled on you, imagine that. Not right away or we would've shut you down as soon as you returned from your weekend getaway. You must've done something to annoy poor Frank."

Ginger tugged on the lapels of her jacket, sniffing. "Of course, as soon as he told us he saw you in Elk Crossing, the same location as Dustin Gantt, we knew something was wrong. The same weekend Liam McCabe mysteriously disappeared, and you never mentioned once to us that you'd been out of town. Maybe if you had, we wouldn't have suspected anything amiss, even after Frank told us where he saw you."

"Really? You wouldn't think anything was amiss that I was in the same place where you murdered Dustin? And how did you kill Samantha?"

"That was you, wasn't it?" Ginger clasped her hands in front of her. "You were wearing that poor girl's sweater the night Garrett died."

"The night you killed him." She jerked her thumb at Mr. Romo. "Does he know you and Garrett were making out on his desk at the moment you killed him?"

Ginger laughed and exchanged a glance with Mr. Romo. "Who do you think gave me the instructions? And as for Samantha, she was a slut who was ready to go home with the first guy she met at the Deluxe. Too bad he happened to work for us."

Mr. Romo stroked his beard. "What organization does Liam McCabe represent? He's too well equipped, too well trained to be on his own. Do you two work for the same agency? Is it the Company?"

"I told you, sweetums. She's here for Sebastian Cole, aren't you? Maybe McCabe is, too. You listen to your brother too much, my love. He's obsessed with Prospero."

Katie pressed her lips into a thin line. "You'd better start thinking of making your way out of here. Can't you hear the explosions? They're coming closer."

"While it would serve you right for betraying our trust

to leave you here in this building while McCabe blows you up, you're more valuable to us alive."

Katie licked her lips. "What do you mean?"

"You do have the kind of skills we need, and after the disaster of this night, we'll need good people to rebuild." Mr. Romo had opened a closet door and dragged out a jacket and a bag.

"What are you talking about? I'm not going to work for you." Her laugh reached an almost hysterical level.

"You will and you'll enjoy it, and you'll enjoy me." He ran a tongue around his full lips. "I haven't forgotten about that aspect of our relationship, either. You'll do what I tell you to do at the computer during the day, and you'll do what I tell you to do in my bed at night."

"You're crazy. That'll never happen. I'd rather see us all blow up first."

Ginger crossed the room and swung open a door next to the windows. A cold gust of wind whooshed into the room.

"What is that? Where does that lead?"

Ginger waved the gun. "To the helipad. We're all taking off and there's not going to be any explosion, at least not for us. Maybe McCabe will just *think* he blew you up. That's good enough for me."

Katie dug her feet into the carpet. She'd ditched her shoes in the stairwell in the hopes that Liam might find them, like Gretel leaving crumbs. "I'm not going anywhere with you."

Ginger strode toward her, smacked her face with the back of her hand and jabbed her in the small of her back with the gun. "Get moving."

Maybe she could jump out of the helicopter, overpower them.

She shuffled toward the door with Ginger prodding her in the back. "I-is there a pilot?"

"Mr. Romo handles the chopper himself."

Romo was slipping into a bomber jacket and slung the bag over his shoulder.

Ginger urged her up the stairs, and when Katie reached the roof, the wind whipped her ponytail across her face.

Mr. Romo joined them as another explosion lit up the night sky. "You keep her here while I start the bird and for God's sake, stay clear of the blades."

He put one foot on the runner and ducked into the chopper. One second later, his body flew backward, knocking into them.

Katie fell to her knees and looked up to see Liam looming in the doorway of the chopper. "Grab the gun, Katie."

Ginger had dropped her weapon, and both women lunged for it at the same time. Ginger's long fingers curled around the handle first, but Katie grabbed the back of Ginger's hair, pulled her head back and then smashed her face against the cement. Ginger's grip slipped off the gun, and it fell over the edge of the roof.

The next explosion rocked the building and threw Katie onto her side.

"Hurry, Katie! Get up. Jump into the chopper. I'm not leaving you."

Ginger was pulling up to her knees, moaning, her face bloody.

Katie hopped to her feet and stepped over her, skirting Mr. Romo's unconscious form.

Liam reached out of the chopper and pulled her inside, flipping switches on the control panel of the bird. As she fell into the seat, she saw Mr. Romo reach for a holster on his calf.

She screamed. "Liam!"

The blades whirred above them and as Mr. Romo staggered to his feet, one of the blades thwacked his back. The next one that hit him knocked him from the roof.

Ginger's keening wail merged with the whine of the chopper as it lifted off.

KATIE'S FINGERS TANGLED with Liam's across the space between their chairs. She didn't exactly know what she was doing here in Florida, but Liam had asked her to come with him, and she'd follow him anywhere.

The door to the office opened behind them, and a tall, angular man strode through it, his energy filling the room, creating tension, excitement.

Liam jumped to his feet. "Sir, this is Katie O'Keefe, the woman I told you about. Katie, this is Jack Coburn, the head of Prospero."

Coburn nodded and slipped into the chair behind his desk, a lock of almost black hair falling over one eye. He pushed it away impatiently. "That was some amazing work you did for us, Katie. Liam's right. He told me all about you."

"Liam's the one who saved the day, or I'd be working for Mr. Romo about now."

"Romo's dead."

She dipped her chin to her chest. "And Ginger Spann?"

"She'll be headed to federal prison once the CIA is finished questioning her." He steepled his fingers and watched them over the top. "Do you know who Mr. Romo was?"

Liam shrugged. "I'd never laid eyes on him the entire time I was there until I kicked him out of his own helicopter."

"You know who Caliban is, right?"

"Was Romo Caliban?" Liam glanced at her. "Caliban is the mysterious head of Tempest. Was that him, sir?"

"We have reason to believe Romo was Caliban's brother."

"Wait." Katie plowed her fingers through her loose hair. "Why is his name Caliban?"

"It's just a codename, a cover, just like Romo." Coburn tipped his chair back and wedged one foot on his desk. "Caliban oversees the entire Tempest organization. We don't know who he is, but Romo came out of nowhere to head up operations of their training facility in Idaho, so we suspect Caliban is a highly placed government official."

"That's what nepotism will get you. Romo didn't do a very good job." Her lips twisted when she recalled the fate he had in store for her.

"A buffoon, more interested in…other things, but he did have an eye for a good programmer, and Liam has been singing your praises ever since we released him from the hospital."

"Where everything was fine, all T-101 out of his system, right?" She took his hand and didn't care if Coburn saw it or not.

"That's right." He squeezed her fingers. "But listen to Jack. He has an offer for you."

"For me?"

"We could use someone with your skills at Prospero, Katie. Would you like to work with us or at least think about it, so this guy—" he jabbed a finger at Liam "—will stop bugging me?"

"I'd love to work for Prospero."

"Thank God. I'm sure you're good, Katie, but mainly we have to make this guy happy. He did a helluva job for us, and we want to keep him around."

"So do I." She grinned like an idiot.

Coburn pushed back from his desk. "This is my office, but it's also my home, and my wife would curse me out in Spanish if I let you go without inviting you to lunch first. So, you two talk it over and join us when you're ready."

As soon as Coburn snapped the door closed behind him, Katie launched out of her chair and landed in Liam's lap. "You did that? You suggested he offer me a position with Prospero?"

"I had to think of some way to keep you close." He wrapped his arms around her waist and kissed her throat.

"Have I ever told you I love you?" She tilted her head, and her wild hair, free from the loathsome ponytails, cascaded over her shoulder.

"You know, I think you let that slip out once by mistake, but just in case it never came out of your mouth again, I committed it to memory."

"You don't have to commit it to your amazing memory, Liam McCabe, because I plan to tell you daily."

He nuzzled her neck. "Mmm, that's okay but I like it better when you show me, but whether you tell me or show me, it doesn't matter because I'm not going anywhere, Katie-O."

She snuggled farther into his lap, showering his face with kisses. She didn't require his assurances anymore, and maybe he didn't require hers, but she never wanted to hold back from this man again. They had each other's backs—and that was coming home.

* * * * *

Read on for a sneak preview of FATAL AFFAIR,
the first book in the FATAL *series*
by New York Times *bestselling author*
Marie Force

ONE

THE SMELL HIT him first.

"Ugh, what the hell is that?" Nick Cappuano dropped his keys into his coat pocket and stepped into the spacious, well-appointed Watergate apartment that his boss, Senator John O'Connor, had inherited from his father.

"Senator!" Nick tried to identify the foul metallic odor. Making his way through the living room, he noticed parts and pieces of the suit John wore yesterday strewn over sofas and chairs, laying a path to the bedroom. He had called the night before to check in with Nick after a dinner meeting with Virginia's Democratic Party leadership, and said he was on his way home. Nick had reminded his thirty-six-year-old boss to set his alarm.

"Senator?" John hated when Nick called him that when they were alone, but Nick insisted the people in John's life afford him the respect of his title.

The odd stench permeating the apartment caused a tingle of anxiety to register on the back of Nick's neck. "John?"

He stepped into the bedroom and gasped. Drenched in blood, John sat up in bed, his eyes open but vacant. A knife spiked through his neck held him in place against the headboard. His hands rested in a pool of blood in his lap.

Gagging, the last thing Nick noticed before he bolted to the bathroom to vomit was that something was hanging out of John's mouth.

Once the violent retching finally stopped, Nick stood

up on shaky legs, wiped his mouth with the back of his hand, and rested against the vanity, waiting to see if there would be more. His cell phone rang. When he didn't take the call, his pager vibrated. Nick couldn't find the where-withal to answer, to say the words that would change ev-erything. *The senator is dead. John's been murdered.* He wanted to go back to when he was still in his car, fuming and under the assumption that his biggest problem that day would be what to do about the man-child he worked for who had once again slept through his alarm.

Thoughts of John, dating back to their first meet-ing in a history class at Harvard freshman year, flashed through Nick's mind, hundreds of snippets spanning a nearly twenty-year friendship. As if to convince himself that his eyes had not deceived him, he leaned forward to glance into the bedroom, wincing at the sight of his best friend—the brother of his heart—stabbed through the neck and covered with blood.

Nick's eyes burned with tears, but he refused to give in to them. Not now. Later maybe, but not now. His phone rang again. This time he reached for it and saw it was Christina, his deputy chief of staff, but didn't take the call. Instead, he dialed 911.

Taking a deep breath to calm his racing heart and mak-ing a supreme effort to keep the hysteria out of his voice, he said, "I need to report a murder." He gave the address and stumbled into the living room to wait for the police, all the while trying to get his head around the image of his dead friend, a visual he already knew would haunt him forever.

Twenty long minutes later, two officers arrived, took a quick look in the bedroom and radioed for backup. Nick was certain neither of them recognized the victim.

He felt as if he was being sucked into a riptide, pulled further and further from the safety of shore, until drawing a breath became a laborious effort. He told the cops exactly what happened—his boss failed to show up for work, he came looking for him and found him dead.

"Your boss's name?"

"United States Senator John O'Connor." Nick watched the two young officers go pale in the instant before they made a second more urgent call for backup.

"Another scandal at the Watergate," Nick heard one of them mutter.

His cell phone rang yet again. This time he reached for it.

"Yeah," he said softly.

"Nick!" Christina cried. "Where the *hell* are you guys? Trevor's having a heart attack!" She referred to their communications director, who had back-to-back interviews scheduled for the senator that morning.

"He's dead, Chris."

"Who's dead? What're you talking about?"

"John."

Her soft cry broke his heart. *"No."* That she was desperately in love with John was no secret to Nick. That she was also a consummate professional who would never act on those feelings was one of the many reasons Nick respected her.

"I'm sorry to just blurt it out like that."

"How?" she asked in a small voice.

"Stabbed in his bed."

Her ravaged moan echoed through the phone. "But who... I mean, *why*?"

"The cops are here, but I don't know anything yet. I need you to request a postponement on the vote."

"I can't," she said, adding in a whisper, "I can't think about that right now."

"You have to, Chris. That bill is his legacy. We can't let all his hard work be for nothing. Can you do it? For him?"

"Yes...okay."

"You have to pull yourself together for the staff, but don't tell them yet. Not until his parents are notified."

"Oh, God, his poor parents. You should go, Nick. It'd be better coming from you than cops they don't know."

"I don't know if I can. How do I tell people I love that their son's been murdered?"

"He'd want it to come from you."

"I suppose you're right. I'll see if the cops will let me."

"What're we going to do without him, Nick?" She posed a question he'd been grappling with himself. "I just can't imagine this world, this *life*, without him."

"I can't either," Nick said, knowing it would be a much different life without John O'Connor at the center of it.

"He's really dead?" she asked as if to convince herself it wasn't a cruel joke. "Someone killed him?"

"Yes."

OUTSIDE THE CHIEF'S office suite, Detective Sergeant Sam Holland smoothed her hands over the toffee-colored hair she corralled into a clip for work, pinched some color into cheeks that hadn't seen the light of day in weeks, and adjusted her gray suit jacket over a red scoop-neck top.

Taking a deep breath to calm her nerves and settle her chronically upset stomach, she pushed open the door and stepped inside. Chief Farnsworth's receptionist greeted her with a smile. "Go right in, Sergeant Holland. He's waiting for you."

Great, Sam thought as she left the receptionist with a weak smile. Before she could give in to the urge to turn tail and run, she erased the grimace from her face and went in.

"Sergeant." The chief, a man she'd once called Uncle Joe, stood up and came around the big desk to greet her with a firm handshake. His gray eyes skirted over her with concern and sympathy, both of which were new since "the incident." She despised being the reason for either. "You look well."

"I feel well."

"Glad to hear it." He gestured for her to have a seat. "Coffee?"

"No, thanks."

Pouring himself a cup, he glanced over his shoulder. "I've been worried about you, Sam."

"I'm sorry for causing you worry and for disgracing the department." This was the first chance she'd had to speak directly to him since she returned from a month of administrative leave, during which she'd practiced the sentence over and over. She thought she'd delivered it with convincing sincerity.

"Sam," he sighed as he sat across from her, cradling his mug between big hands. "You've done nothing to disgrace yourself or the department. Everyone makes mistakes."

"Not everyone makes mistakes that result in a dead child, Chief."

He studied her for a long, intense moment as if he was making some sort of decision. "Senator John O'Connor was found murdered in his apartment this morning."

"Jesus," she gasped. "How?"

"I don't have all the details, but from what I've been told so far, it appears he was dismembered and stabbed through the neck. Apparently, his chief of staff found him."

"Nick," she said softly.

"Excuse me?"

"Nick Cappuano is O'Connor's chief of staff."

"You know him?"

"Knew him. Years ago," she added, surprised and unsettled to discover the memory of him still had power over her, that just the sound of his name rolling off her lips could make her heart race.

"I'm assigning the case to you."

Surprised at being thrust so forcefully back into the real work she had craved since her return to duty, she couldn't help but ask, "Why me?"

"Because you need this, and so do I. We both need a win."

The press had been relentless in its criticism of him, of her, of the department, but to hear him acknowledge it made her ache. Her father had come up through the ranks with Farnsworth, which was probably the number one reason why she still had a job. "Is this a test? Find out who killed the senator and my previous sins are forgiven?"

He put down his coffee cup and leaned forward, elbows resting on knees. "The only person who needs to forgive you, Sam, is you."

Infuriated by the surge of emotion brought on by his softly spoken words, Sam cleared her throat and stood up. "Where does O'Connor live?"

"The Watergate. Two uniforms are already there. Crime scene is on its way." He handed her a slip of paper with the address. "I don't have to tell you that this needs to be handled with the utmost discretion."

He also didn't have to tell her that this was the only chance she'd get at redemption.

"Won't the Feds want in on this?"

"They might, but they don't have jurisdiction, and they know it. They'll be breathing down my neck, though, so report directly to me. I want to know everything ten minutes after you do. I'll smooth it with Stahl," he added, referring to the lieutenant she usually answered to.

Heading for the door, she said, "I won't let you down."

"You never have before."

With her hand resting on the door handle, she turned back to him. "Are you saying that as the chief of police or as my Uncle Joe?"

His face lifted into a small but sincere smile. "Both."

TWO

Sitting on John's sofa under the watchful eyes of the two policemen, Nick's mind raced with the staggering number of things that needed to be done, details to be seen to, people to call. His cell phone rang relentlessly, but he ignored it after deciding he would talk to no one until he had seen John's parents. Almost twenty years ago they took an instant shine to the hard-luck scholarship student their son brought home from Harvard for a weekend visit and made him part of their family. Nick owed them so much, not the least of which was hearing the news of their son's death from him if possible.

He ran his hand through his hair. "How much longer?"

"Detectives are on their way."

Ten minutes later, Nick heard her before he saw her. A flurry of activity and a burst of energy preceded the detectives' entrance into the apartment. He suppressed a groan. *Wasn't it enough that his friend and boss had been murdered? He had to face her, too? Weren't there thousands of District cops? Was she really the only one available?*

Sam came into the apartment, oozing authority and competence. In light of her recent troubles, Nick couldn't believe she had any of either left. "Get some tape across that door," she ordered one of the officers. "Start a log with a timeline of who got here when. No one comes in or goes out without my okay, got it?"

"Yes, ma'am. The Patrol sergeant is on his way along with Deputy Chief Conklin and Detective Captain Malone."

"Let me know when they get here." Without so much as a glance in his direction, Nick watched her stalk through the apartment and disappear into the bedroom. Following her, a handsome young detective with bed head nodded to Nick.

He heard the murmur of voices from the bedroom and saw a camera flash. They emerged fifteen minutes later, both noticeably paler. For some reason, Nick was gratified to know the detectives working the case weren't so jaded as to be unaffected by what they'd just seen.

"Start a canvass of the building," Sam ordered her partner. "Where the hell is Crime Scene?"

"Hung up at another homicide," one of the other officers replied.

She finally turned to Nick, nothing in her pale blue eyes indicating that she recognized or remembered him. But the fact that she didn't introduce herself or ask for his name told him she knew exactly who he was. "We'll need your prints."

"They're on file," he mumbled. "Congressional background check."

She wrote something in the small notebook she tugged from the back pocket of gray, form-fitting pants. There were years on her gorgeous face that hadn't been there the last time he'd had the opportunity to look closely, and he couldn't tell if her hair was as long as it used to be since it was twisted into a clip. The curvy body and endless legs hadn't changed at all.

"No forced entry," she noted. "Who has a key?"

"Who *doesn't* have a key?"

"I'll need a list. You have a key, I assume."

Nick nodded. "That's how I got in."

"Was he seeing anyone?"

"No one serious, but he had no trouble attracting female companionship." Nick didn't add that John's casual approach to women and sex had been a source of tension between the two men, with Nick fearful that John's social life would one day lead to political trouble. He hadn't imagined it might also lead to murder.

"When was the last time you saw him?"

"When he left the office for a dinner meeting with the Virginia Democrats last night. Around six-thirty or so."

"Spoke to him?"

"Around ten when he said he was on his way home."

"Alone?"

"He didn't say, and I didn't ask."

"Take me through what happened this morning."

He told her about Christina trying to reach John, beginning at seven, and of coming to the apartment expecting to find the senator once again sleeping through his alarm.

"So this has happened before?"

"No, he's never been murdered before."

Her expression was anything but amused. "Do you think this is funny, Mr. Cappuano?"

"Hardly. My best friend is dead, Sergeant. A United States senator has been murdered. There's nothing funny about that."

"Which is why you need to answer the questions and save the droll humor for a more appropriate time."

Chastened, Nick said, "He slept through his alarm and ringing telephones at least once, if not twice, a month."

"Did he drink?"

"Socially, but I rarely saw him drunk."

"Prescription drugs? Sleeping pills?"

Nick shook his head. "He was just a very heavy sleeper."

"And it fell to his chief of staff to wake him up? There wasn't anyone else you could send?"

"The senator valued his privacy. There've been occasions when he wasn't alone, and neither of us felt his love life should be the business of his staff."

"But he didn't care if you knew who he was sleeping with?"

"He knew he could count on my discretion." He looked up, unprepared for the punch to the gut that occurred when his eyes met hers. Her unsettled expression made him wonder if she felt it, too. "His parents need to be notified. I'd like to be the one to tell them."

Sam studied him for a long moment. "I'll arrange it. Where are they?"

"At their farm in Leesburg. It needs to be soon. We're postponing a vote we worked for months to get to. It'll be all over the news that something's up."

"What's the vote for?"

He told her about the landmark immigration bill and John's role as the co-sponsor.

With a curt nod, she walked away.

AN HOUR LATER, Nick was a passenger in an unmarked Metropolitan Police SUV, headed west to Leesburg with Sam at the wheel. She'd left her partner with a staggering list of instructions and insisted on accompanying Nick to tell John's parents.

"Do you need something to eat?"

He shook his head. No way could he even think about eating—not with the horrific task he had ahead of him. Besides, his stomach hadn't recovered from the earlier bout of vomiting.

"You know, we could still call the Loudoun County Police or the Virginia State Police to handle this," she said for the second time.

"No."

After an awkward silence, she said, "I'm sorry this happened to your friend and that you had to see him that way."

"Thank you."

"Are you going to answer that?" she asked of his relentless cell phone.

"No."

"How about you turn it off then? I can't stand listening to a ringing phone."

Reaching for his belt, he grabbed his cell phone, his emotions still raw after watching John be taken from his apartment in a body bag. Before he shut the cell phone off, he called Christina.

"Hey," she said, her voice heavy with relief and emotion. "I've been trying to reach you."

"Sorry." Pulling his tie loose and releasing his top button, he cast a sideways glance at Sam, whose warm, feminine fragrance had overtaken the small space inside the car. "I was dealing with cops."

"Where are you now?"

"On my way to Leesburg."

"God," Christina sighed. "I don't envy you that. Are you okay?"

"Never better."

"I'm sorry. Dumb question."

"It's okay. Who knows what we're supposed to say or do in this situation. Did you postpone the vote?"

"Yes, but Martin and McDougal are having an apoplexy," she said, meaning John's co-sponsor on the bill and the Democratic majority leader. "They're demanding to know what's going on."

"Hold them off. Another hour. Maybe two. Same thing with the staff. I'll give you the green light as soon as I've told his parents."

"I will. Everyone knows something's up because the Capitol Police posted an officer outside John's office and won't let anyone in there."

"It's because the cops are waiting for a search warrant," Nick told her.

"Why do they need a warrant to search the victim's office?"

"Something about chain of custody with evidence and pacifying the Capitol Police."

"Oh, I see. I was thinking we should have Trevor draft a statement so we're ready."

"That's why I called."

"We'll get on it." She sounded relieved to have something to do.

"Are you okay with telling Trevor? Want me to do it?"

"I think I can do it, but thanks for asking."

"How're you holding up?" he asked.

"I'm in total shock…all that promise and potential just gone…" She began to weep again. "It's going to hurt like hell when the shock wears off."

"Yeah," he said softly. "No doubt."

"I'm here if you need anything."

"Me, too, but I'm going to shut the phone off for a while. It's been ringing nonstop."

"I'll email the statement to you when we have it done."

"Thanks, Christina. I'll call you later." Nick ended the call and took a look at his recent email messages, hardly surprised by the outpouring of dismay and concern over the postponement of the vote. One was from Senator Martin himself—*What the fuck is going on, Cappuano?*

Sighing, he turned off the cell phone and dropped it into his coat pocket.

"Was that your girlfriend?" Sam asked, startling him.

"No, my deputy."

"Oh."

Wondering what she was getting at, he added, "We work closely together. We're good friends."

"Why are you being so defensive?"

"What's your *problem*?" he asked.

"I don't have a problem. You're the one with problems."

"So all that great press you've been getting lately hasn't been a problem for you?"

"Why, Nick, I didn't realize you cared."

"I don't."

"Yes, you made that very clear."

He spun halfway around in the seat to stare at her. "*Are you for real?* You're the one who didn't return any of my calls."

She glanced over at him, her face flat with surprise. "What calls?"

After staring at her in disbelief for a long moment, he settled back in his seat and fixed his eyes on the cars sharing the Interstate with them.

A few minutes passed in uneasy silence.

"What calls, Nick?"

"I called you," he said softly. "For days after that night, I tried to reach you."

"I didn't know," she stammered. "No one told me."

"It doesn't matter now. It was a long time ago." But if his reaction to seeing her again after six years of thinking about her was any indication, it *did* matter. It mattered a lot.

*Continue reading Sam and Nick's story in
FATAL AFFAIR, available in print and ebook
from Carina Press.*

REQUEST YOUR FREE BOOKS!
2 FREE NOVELS PLUS 2 FREE GIFTS!

H️ HARLEQUIN®

INTRIGUE

BREATHTAKING ROMANTIC SUSPENSE

YES! Please send me 2 FREE Harlequin® Intrigue novels and my 2 FREE gifts (gifts are worth about $10). After receiving them, if I don't wish to receive any more books, I can return the shipping statement marked "cancel." If I don't cancel, I will receive 6 brand-new novels every month and be billed just $4.74 per book in the U.S. or $5.49 per book in Canada. That's a savings of at least 12% off the cover price! It's quite a bargain! Shipping and handling is just 50¢ per book in the U.S. and 75¢ per book in Canada.* I understand that accepting the 2 free books and gifts places me under no obligation to buy anything. I can always return a shipment and cancel at any time. Even if I never buy another book, the two free books and gifts are mine to keep forever.

182/382 HDN GH3D

Name _____

(PLEASE PRINT)

Address _____ Apt. # _____

City _____ State/Prov. _____ Zip/Postal Code _____

Signature (if under 18, a parent or guardian must sign) _____

Mail to the **Reader Service:**
IN U.S.A.: P.O. Box 1867, Buffalo, NY 14240-1867
IN CANADA: P.O. Box 609, Fort Erie, Ontario L2A 5X3

**Are you a subscriber to Harlequin® Intrigue books
and want to receive the larger-print edition?
Call 1-800-873-8635 or visit www.ReaderService.com.**

* Terms and prices subject to change without notice. Prices do not include applicable taxes. Sales tax applicable in N.Y. Canadian residents will be charged applicable taxes. Offer not valid in Quebec. This offer is limited to one order per household. Not valid for current subscribers to Harlequin Intrigue books. All orders subject to credit approval. Credit or debit balances in a customer's account(s) may be offset by any other outstanding balance owed by or to the customer. Please allow 4 to 6 weeks for delivery. Offer available while quantities last.

Your Privacy—The Reader Service is committed to protecting your privacy. Our Privacy Policy is available online at www.ReaderService.com or upon request from the Reader Service.

We make a portion of our mailing list available to reputable third parties that offer products we believe may interest you. If you prefer that we not exchange your name with third parties, or if you wish to clarify or modify your communication preferences, please visit us at www.ReaderService.com/consumerchoice or write to us at Reader Service Preference Service, P.O. Box 9062, Buffalo, NY 14240-9062. Include your complete name and address.

SPECIAL EXCERPT FROM

H HARLEQUIN®

INTRIGUE

*When a beautiful rancher's past threatens to take a
deadly turn, her best chance of surviving is with the
help of the sexy Texas Ranger she never thought she'd
see again—or have to tell she's pregnant with his baby!*

*Read on for a sneak preview of LONE WOLF LAWMAN,
the first book in* USA TODAY *bestselling author*
Delores Fossen's *gripping new miniseries*
APPALOOSA PASS RANCH.

The silence came. Addie, staring at him. Obviously
trying to make sense of this. He wanted to tell her there
was nothing about this that made sense because they
were dealing with a very dangerous, crazy man.

"Oh, God," she finally said.

Now, her fear was sky high, and Weston held his
breath. He didn't expect Addie to go blindly along with
a plan to stop her father. But she did want to stop the
Moonlight Strangler from claiming another victim.

Weston was counting heavily on that.

However, Addie shook her head. "I can't help you."

That sure wasn't the reaction Weston had expected.
He'd figured Addie was as desperate to end this as he was.

She squeezed her eyes shut a moment. "I'll get my
mother, and we can go to the sheriff's office. Two of my
brothers are there, and they can make sure this monster
stays far away from us."

"You'll be safe at the sheriff's office," Weston agreed,
"but you can't stay there forever. Neither can your family.

Eventually, you'll have to leave, and the killer will come after you."

"That can't happen!" Addie groaned and looked up at the ceiling as if she expected some kind of divine help. "I can't be in that kind of danger."

Weston tried to keep his voice as calm as possible. Hard to do, though, with the emotions swirling like a tornado inside him. "I'm sorry. If there was another way to stop him, then I wouldn't have come here. I know I don't have a right to ask, but I need your help."

"I can't."

"You can't? Convince me why," Weston snapped. "Because I'm not getting this. You must want this killer off the street. It's the only way you'll ever be truly safe."

Addie opened her mouth. Closed it. And she stared at him. "I'd planned on telling you. Not like this. But if I ever saw you again, I intended to tell you."

There was a new emotion in her voice and on her face. One that Weston couldn't quite put his finger on. "Tell me what?" he asked.

She dragged in a long breath and straightened her shoulders. "I can't be bait for the Moonlight Strangler because I can't risk being hurt." Addie took another deep breath. "I'm three months pregnant. And the baby is *yours*."

Don't miss
LONE WOLF LAWMAN
by USA TODAY *bestselling author Delores Fossen,*
available August 2015 wherever
Harlequin Intrigue® books and ebooks are sold.

www.Harlequin.com

Limited time offer!

$1.⁰⁰ OFF

Mixing romance and politics can be fatal in the *New York Times* bestselling *Fatal Series* by

MARIE FORCE

Fall for fast-paced political intrigue, gritty suspense and a romance that makes headlines.

Save $1.00 on any one book in
The Fatal Series!

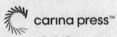 carina press™

www.CarinaPress.com
www.TheFatalSeries.com

$1.⁰⁰ OFF

the purchase price of any book in
The Fatal Series by Marie Force.

Offer valid from September 15, 2015, to October 19, 2015. Redeemable at participating retail outlets. Limit one coupon per purchase. Valid in the USA and Canada only.

52613005

Canadian Retailers: Harlequin Enterprises Limited will pay the face value of this coupon plus 10.25¢ if submitted by customer for this product only. Any other use constitutes fraud. Coupon is nonassignable. Void if taxed, prohibited or restricted by law. Consumer must pay any government taxes. Void if copied. Inmar Promotional Services ("IPS") customers submit coupons and proof of sales to Harlequin Enterprises Limited, P.O. Box 3000, Saint John, NB E2L 4L3, Canada. Non-IPS retailer—for reimbursement submit coupons and proof of sales directly to Harlequin Enterprises Limited, Retail Marketing Department, 225 Duncan Mill Rd., Don Mills, Ontario M3B 3K9, Canada.

5 65373 00076 2 (8100)0 12092

U.S. Retailers: Harlequin Enterprises Limited will pay the face value of this coupon plus 8¢ if submitted by customer for this product only. Any other use constitutes fraud. Coupon is nonassignable. Void if taxed, prohibited or restricted by law. Consumer must pay any government taxes. Void if copied. For reimbursement submit coupons and proof of sales directly to Harlequin Enterprises Limited, P.O. Box 880478, El Paso, TX 88588-0478, U.S.A. Cash value 1/100 cents.

® and ™ are trademarks owned and used by the trademark owner and/or its licensee.

© 2015 Harlequin Enterprises Limited

CARMFHI00257COUP

Turn your love of reading into rewards you'll love with
Harlequin My Rewards

THE WORLD IS BETTER WITH

Romance

Harlequin has everything from contemporary, passionate and heartwarming to suspenseful and inspirational stories.

Whatever your mood, we have a romance just for you!

Connect with us to find your next great read, special offers and more.

f /HarlequinBooks

🐦 @HarlequinBooks

www.HarlequinBlog.com

www.Harlequin.com/Newsletters

◆ HARLEQUIN®

A *Romance* FOR EVERY MOOD™

www.Harlequin.com